TATTERED

CARIETTA DORSCH

This book is for entertainment purposes only.
Library of Congress Control Number: 2024944148
Printed in United States of America
ISBN: 9798894670133

Dedication

To my mother, the unwavering source of love, support, and inspiration in my life. I hope it makes you proud. With all my love and appreciation, thank you for being my rock, my mentor, and my best friend.

With much appreciation, thank you Brian Katcher.

Thanks to Christina Marie, for your unwavering support and friendship.

Thanks to Marie Lestrange for being such a great friend.

And, thank you to all those trips I took to the movie store and theater as a teenager.

Tattered is a work of fiction. The characters, incidents, and dialog are drawn from the author's imagination and are not to be construed as accurate. Any resemblance to actual events or persons, living or dead, is entirely coincidental.

1

I sit where I am for a little while, head down, hair frizzed wildly in the back, my fingers laced loosely between my thighs.

Breathe easy.

I keep telling myself that, repeating it like a mystical incantation. I could use the help. The last time I tried to speak, I just couldn't. I released a pent-up breath in a gusty sigh and braced myself for a wave of relief. Relief did come, but not in the tidal wave I had hoped.

Breathe easy.

My voice came this time. It was slightly watery but audible and mostly under control. My stomach doesn't just do flips; it does high-wire somersaults without any safety net.

Yes, I understand.

I can do this.

Breathe easy.

There's no better place to start than the beginning. I know you're asking yourself why…how…but bear with me– it's all important.

I'm sharing my story here with all its perplexities and imperfections. It's not a tale of facts and events that will one day make a shitty Lifetime movie. Still, of my personal experience, it is my story, in my words, even though it could all be described so well by Hannibal Lecter's question to Jodie Foster: Are you strong enough to point that high-powered perception at yourself? What about it? Why don't you- why don't you look at yourself and write down what you see? Or maybe you're afraid to.

I was afraid to do so for the longest time, but not now. I need to share this, so trust me, it's all important.

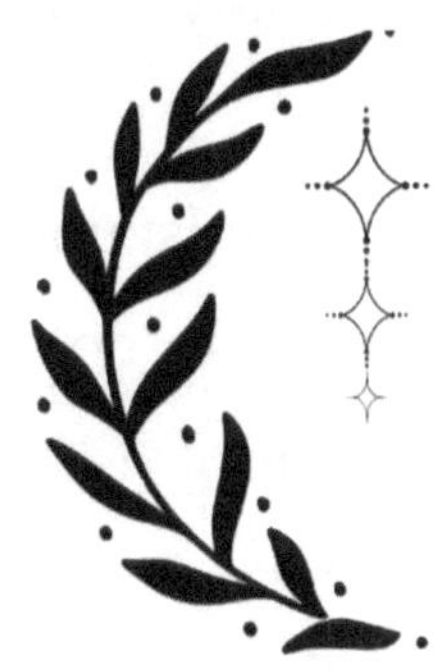

My name is Salem Moon Richardson. I've been on my own since my dad died. I was only seventeen, and even though three years have passed… it still hurts. I guess I'd be what they call a daddy's girl. I can still see my dad's quick grin, his lively eyes, the way his hands moved restlessly when he talked.

What I *can't* see is him using those hands to hold the shotgun steady and pull the trigger– no matter how many times I try.

My mother drove him to that point by living her own *Trainspottin* mixed with *Spun* and just a pinch of *Requiem for a Dream*. She came home late one night. We had been up for hours waiting for her and on the verge of calling the police. She stumbled in the door and fell to the ground almost instantly.

My mother had been beaten so severely that I first thought it was some strange woman on our living room floor. She tearfully admitted her addiction and that she'd slept with many men, and she'dn that had beaten her to keep it up.

Looking at her bloodstained clothes and battered face, my dad just started to cry. He realized then that this wasn't something new. It had been going on for a long time and he wondered why and questioned how he missed all of her little desperate signals. She had kept so many secrets behind her cheery demeanor and sunny smile. Had he known, could he have helped?

She left us and died shortly after because she couldn't afford any rehab. She had just enough money to buy an expensive umbrella, but unfortunately, not enough for medical care.

My dad took his own life precisely four days after my mother died. I was a week away from being eighteen. The image of him slumped between the recliner and ottoman in a pool of his own blood, the ceiling still dripping….it will forever be imprinted in my nightmares.

It still haunts me.

I mourned but in my own way. I didn't have time to throw my hands in the air and give up. I couldn't ask Doc to lend me the DeLorean so I could push the pedal to 88 miles an hour.

I was on my own. I didn't have time to hide in

the dark and wish it all away. I had to take it for what it was and keep moving forward. In a way, I feel like I would've made my dad proud of that.

As for my mother, I still loved her; it was just… any woman who would fuck around on her husband just for a cheap fix, and I just wasn't able to look up to her. I lost all respect and admiration for my mother, and she became everything I never wanted to be as a woman.

Of course, my school grades dropped as depression took its toll, but I kept going. I mechanically did everything I was expected to do, but it wasn't enjoyable anymore.

I was existing– not living.

It was during this time in my life when I discovered the healing powers of marijuana.

Insert…happiness.

It was just a half-hearted rolled joint of mid-grade weed that I had to sneak off behind the football field bleachers to smoke, but I sure fell in love with it. This is what helped me finish school instead of simply dropping out. So, unlike what people see in *Up in Smoke*, *Friday*, or any of Kevin Smith's films, I used the high to cope with my struggles and ease the pain.

This habit is what first fueled my search for a

job. Well, that…and I actually had a need for one.

After working a few odd and end jobs throughout my last year of high school, I could finally look for a full-time job with a full-time paycheck. The bills for my apartment weren't anything close to the first few bills I had to pay while I stayed in what was once our family house, and that was a good thing. If I remember correctly, I could only make it three months of paying all the bills before I realized it was *way* too much for me to keep up with. My dad's insurance and the money I got for the house were enough to get by for a while–but I still needed a job.

Which brings me to the movies.

All I knew, all I know, I learned from movies.

But a scene of real life struggle is not the same as living it, and a thousand scenes of happiness do not make you happy. I've seen many more movies than just about anybody, but none prepared me for this.

I learned after my parents had passed that misery was a choice. If you allow the events that transpired to intrude on your own happiness…well, then it's really your own fault.

Yes, it hurt like hell. It felt like a piece of me died with them, but the fact was… I was not dead, so I had to find that missing piece to get my shit together and be the best me I could be.

I know my dad would've liked that.

This job search is what led me to the Casanova Theater in downtown Asheboro on Sunset Avenue.

The how, the when, the what, it all starts here.

Quiet on set. Roll the camera.

TATTERED

2

Breathe easy.

It's getting difficult to do that.

I run my fingers through my hair without really thinking about it, but when I bring my hand down, it's wet.

Why is it wet?

I grasp my other hand in an attempt to let them comfort each other in my lap. Or at least I tried to.

Breathe easy.

My lower lip trembles, and I look up. A tear runs down my cheek with another threatening to fall.

I'm trying to get my thoughts together.

I'm sorry.

Breathe easy.

I stared at the sullen face looking back at me in the mirror and tried to decide whether or not it needed makeup or not. I've never been the type of girl to wear a lot anyway, but today was important.

It was my job interview.

A little eyeliner around my dark green eyes wouldn't hurt, I decided. Once I applied the right touch, my lips were up next. They were full and a naturally soft pink, but the longer I soaked in my vampire of a complexion, it was clear I needed a little more color. If they were doing another casting call for some new *Twilight* knock-off, I'd be good to go.

But no. So I reached for a tube of lip gloss.

My hair only got the quick hand fluff treatment. I was lucky enough to have this chocolate wave, a mixture of Dad's hair color and the slightly curled look from my Mom. I wore it long and rarely put it up unless it was really hot outside or if I was cooking.

"All right, Mr. DeMille … I'm ready for my close-up," I cooed, blowing a kiss at the mirror.

I put on my low-top Converse, even though my five-six height didn't need any enhancement today. Then, I made a circuit around my apartment. It wasn't much of a self-paced tour … I only do it to check everything. Yay, OCD!

Not.

My place had a living room, a bathroom, and kitchen. The kitchen was just an alcove with a sink and a too-small fridge. I hadn't bothered to decorate much, unless you count the bookshelves that lined the wall top to bottom with DVDs and Blue-Ray, and even a few old-school VHS (but those were just for looks). One last check that every was unplugged and in its place, and I headed out the door.

Zoo Parkway took me downtown, and then I cut up to Highway 64 after passing the CVS Pharmacy. Traffic in Asheboro can be the great American nightmare in any part of downtown, but this morning was particularly bad. Stuck behind a wreck ahead, I went over what I may be asked in the interview and what I would like to ask the theater manager.

Once I turned on Fayetteville I could see on the left the bank's clock tower signaling that I was close to Sunset Avenue. I took a deep breath when I stopped at the curb, watching a couple of city workers. Before stepping out of my car I took one more glance at my phone to check the time.

Now, I was standing in front of the Casanova Theater, looking at the sign that hung on chains above the ticket booth.

WATCH YOUR DREAMS COME TRUE!

It was as if seeing a better world was a goal attainable by any reasonable, hardworking consumer who bought a ticket for it.

Riiiight.

I had my doubts about that, but I've always been enthralled by the power of a good movie and even more mesmerized by the impact of a great one. My father had gotten me started down the movie buff path ever since he showed me his favorite … *The Big Lebowski.* Through him I learned any movie, every film that you see in your lifetime, has a soul. The soul of the movie came from the people who created it, starred in it, and for those who sat down to watch it.

Every time someone chooses to watch it again, the spirit of the film changes and grows, and this is how classics are born. Born into timeless films that were watched forever.

I met John Kimbrall as I was walking up to the front door. He was reading and picking his nose at the same time. After a few preliminary explorations, his finger went for another dive in his nose… knuckle-deep. He examined it, then parked it under the booth.

Gross.

"Didn't pack any lunch?" I asked in my best

bitch voice.

He was startled to such a degree that he could easily have been mistaken for a complete idiot.

"Sorry." He muttered, cheeks now a bright red of embarrassment. His expression that followed instantly made me feel bad.

"It's okay." I chided, "As long as you share. I forgot to get lunch, too."

"John," he said while reaching a hand toward the opening in the booth's window before retracting it. "Yeah, ya probably don't trust my hands."

"Nor your feet." I laughed. His joking manner rubbed off on me.

His teeth were stained, either from cigarettes or coffee. But that didn't matter … John's yellowed teeth weren't the reason I was here.

"So … I'm here for a job interview. Are you in charge?"

"Nope." He shook his head. "I'm the fixer. When the popcorn stops a poppin' or the toilets start flushin' in reverse, I'm your guy." He pointed a thumb to his chest with pride. "The manager is Steve Hodges. He should be in his office, which is the only office in this place. It's next to the bathrooms."

I chuckled. "Must be a great view."

"Oh yeah."

"How would I get to this prestigious office?"

"Besides following the smell," he smiled, "go past the snack bar and take the left hallway. The right leads you to the seats. There are only four doors, and this is marked with a fancy plastic sign on the door with his name."

"Thanks."

I heard the great nose-miner John laugh to himself as I pulled on a door that said push to open. Honestly, I'd have laughed at myself, too, if I wasn't so anxious about getting this job. The further I stepped in, the more my nostrils were assaulted by the smell of years' worth of popcorn drowning in butter. Spilled sodas and sugary sweets topped off the stench. Fluorescent lights gave the room a soft hum one only hears when all is quiet. The main floor was divided equally. On the left the concession stand with the usual snack bar that had a variety of snacks, drinks and candy on display. On the right, two pinball machines sat next to a lone gumball machine, the kind that you cranked a quarter in and watched your gumball twirl down a series of loops. Classic movie posters covered the walls; I saw Marlon

Brando portraying the Godfather and Al Pacino telling the viewer to 'say hello to his little friend' as he pointed his M16. I even saw Anthony Perkins dressed as Bates' mother and Clint Eastwood pointed in the direction I needed to go with Joe Kidd's pistol.

On my way past the snack bar, a rustling of boxes and muttered obscenities (*fuck* the clearest one of all) caught my attention. A young woman jerked up with yet another fuck escaping her lips, and she quickly slapped a hand over her mouth when she saw me.

"Sorry," she said, removing her hand from her mouth. "It's alright. I think I heard that word before. I'm just not sure where." I joked, trying to loosen my wound-up nerves.

"Elmo taught me."

"Really?" My eyebrow raised with the question.

"Wait, no. He was trying to spell 'truck'. Silly me." She waved her hand in a shooing gesture as if the subject were a bothersome fly. "So, you're the new girl here?" she asked while adjusting her glasses, trying her best to make a strand of her unruly black hair stay tucked behind her ear. I learned later that her name was Matty Conn.

"Hopefully, I have an interview with Mr.

Hodges."

"Oh, Steve's in his office; well, he should be. I think he and Chan are done with fixing a few chairs."

"He was helping?" I asked, surprised.

"Yeah, he helps out a lot around here. He's a pretty good boss." She was opening a Twix wrapper while trying to hold the drink cup under the fountain's fall of Sprite. Two fingers on the button to dispense it, with three wrapped around her cookie-like candy bar. "Down the hall that way, last door on the left." She pointed down the same hall Clint was. "Good luck." She took a bite of Twix and a sip of Sprite simultaneously.

"Thanks." I said over my shoulder as I continued on toward the interview. I tried not to let my nerves get the best of me but failed at keeping them under control completely. A slight dampness was developing under my arms, and it was slightly more difficult to catch a deep breath.

I can do this, I told myself.

I passed the first door on the left, which had to be their janitorial closet. The next two doors were side by side on the right. Those must be the elusive restrooms I learned about earlier. The men's had a picture of Harrison Ford's Han Solo underneath the sign. On the women's, a picture of Carrie Fisher's Princess Leia, with a nearly unnoticeable piece of graffiti under it. In small letters, someone had written, RIP.

I crept as quiet as a cat on the hunt, even though I was as nervous as a cat in a dog house, inching closer to the door of Hodges' office, which was already slightly ajar. I straightened my back and blew out a deep breath I hadn't realized I was holding.

When I raised my fist to knock on the door I noticed a chip missing from my painted purple index fingernail and hoped this little flaw didn't make me look like I didn't take care of myself.

"Come in," Hodges called out after one knock.

I made my way in and started to close the door when he said, "Just leave it open."

Oh shit.

This can't be good. Leaving the door open meant he planned on making this quick.

I know it's silly now, but at the moment I thought he saw my chipped fingernail polish and had already judged harshly.

My concerns vanished almost at the same time as they formed. "Sorry 'bout the heat. My office fan broke yesterday."

"It's okay." I said.

He ran his hand through his hair. Hmmm. I wondered if his hairline was receding or if it was just thin. He tried the fans' on switch one more time in an attempt to enjoy the pleasures of the spinning blades but then gave up. "Well, which one is this about?" he asked with his focus back on me.

"Which one...wait, what?"

"Job. I have two openings. Ticket booth or projector." He seemed nice, but a little on edge.

My lips parted to answer, but then he interrupted me, then he interrupted me. "Before you answer, just know that's your main job, but I run a very small, close-knit group, so you'll help out anywhere that's needed."

"Okay," I bit my lower lip, shifting my weight on either foot and avoiding his stern gaze. "I'd like the projector, but I don't know how to-"

He raised a hand, cracking the harsh facade with a small smile. "That's alright. I'll teach ya." He opened the drawer, pulled out a sheet of paper, plucked a pen from a cup, and placed both in front of me. "Read and sign." He pointed at the places my name should go.

"I got the job?" I asked, a little doubtful, but mostly perplexed.

"Yeah, you got the job."

"Thank you very much, Sir," I said.

"No problem, I was determined to hire someone. I even told myself, 'I'm gonna make him an offer he can't refuse.'"

"Well," I smiled, "if you build it, they will come."

He laughed. "True, true. I believe you'll do very well here."

My heart thumped in my ribcage like an angry bird in a cage trying to escape. Holy crap! I did it! I got the job! I got a fucking job!

I got a fucking job!

Now, it was time to treat myself to a little congratulatory present. I pulled into the parking lot of Asheboro Pawn, planning to buy some DVDs to watch tonight. It had formerly been a pet shop, but that was when I was very young. The front plate-glass window still has a shadow of the past with a barely noticeable

'Pets R Friends' stenciled underneath the now '$BuySell Trade $.' I've been going there for as long as I could recall– almost every weekend. My dad used to come with me, but after a while, he trusted me enough not only to go alone but with the choices I made.

Asheboro Pawn is a small, family-owned shop. I've seen the father, but the mother is the owner, and her two daughters and son are always behind the counter, ready to help.

The door chimed to alert them that a customer was entering the store. I was welcomed by four identical, white smiles.

"Welcome back, welcome back," one daughter said.

"Movie-girl," the other daughter laughed.

"That's me." I smiled back at them.

"Lots of new movies for you," said the mother.

"Great, thanks."

I turned from the counter and went to the back. For almost half an hour, I wandered within the winding labyrinth of metal racks, breathing in the smell of the plastic cases. I let my hand brush across the spines of the DVDs, musing over what my choice would be for tonight. On the wall next to the shelves were TVs, stereos, and a variety of other electronics. On one of the display TVs, they were showing *Inside Out.*

As I searched the shelf, my eyes hunted for titles that grabbed my attention. I found a Bill Murray I hadn't seen, *Rock the Kasbah.* It also had Zooey Deschanel staring in it. I pulled out *American Carnage* and *The Fallout* to look at, both of which had one of my newest favorites in it, Jenna Ortega, so I chose them to buy. I paid for my purchases and went home.

I got a job!

TATTERED

3

Breathe easy.

These words keep running through my head-recycling themselves like an endless tape-loop.

Without my voice to break it, the silence is as thick as the dust under library shelves.

I run my tongue across my lower lip but flinch from the sharp pain and taste of iron.

Do I have to tell you all of this right now?

My lips give another tremble, my eye another tear.

Yeah, I guess I do.

Breathe easy...

breathe easy.

I woke up that morning to an empty bowl and only the smell of marijuana left in the baggie. I picked up my phone while I made coffee and called my pot dealer, Amy. Now, I was standing at her apartment door, waiting for her to answer the bell.

"Sup," Amy said, opening her door.

"What's up?"

Her hair was long and brown with blue tips. She had piercings in her lower lip and left nostril. Her black jeans were so tight, they appeared painted on, and her sleeveless shirt sported the saying: I'M NOT A LESBIAN, BUT MYGIRLFRIEND IS.

The apartment smelled of soap, paint, and freshly brewed coffee. It was clinically clean. I followed her in and sat on one of the two stools by a small table in the hall. The apartment felt more like a cramped room with a hall.

Amy lit a cigarette, blew smoke from her nose, and tapped the ash into a Coke can I was hoping was empty.

"Hold on one sec, this is my favorite kill," she nodded toward the television mounted on the wall.

We watched Sarah Michelle Gellar run toward the store, being chased by the man in the rain-slicker and his deadly hook.

Once Helen's dying screams were drowned out by the parade, she asked, "How much do you need?"

"You got a dime?" I asked.

"Always," she smirked. She loved to provoke and flirt with me. She pulled a scale out, a box of clear baggies with the lock seal, and a bigger bag full of marijuana. She started pulling off pieces from the big clump and putting them in a baggie, every so often using the scale. Finally, she got the baggie to weigh a tenth of an ounce.

"Here you are, Salem Moon," she purred.

I smiled, "Thanks. Do you always use the middle name?"

"It sounds cooler that way. It reminds me of anime."

"That's me the coolest, even though I'm not a cartoon," I laughed.

"Well, thanks. Wish I could stay, but I got work in a little bit, maybe next time."

"For sure, I got the *Friday the 13th* box set the other day and a new bong."

"I can't today, even though that does sound tempting, but you know I'll be back."

"Be careful with that stuff,, or else you'll be thinking you're a cartoon Salem Moon," she laughed.

"Oh, I will. Have a good day," I said, smiling back.

"I will, I'll probably just binge *Wednesday* and crush on Jenna Ortega or maybe Kiernan Shipka in *Chilling Adventures of Sabrina.*" I headed out the door and decided to check out the park and enjoy the sunshine.

It was pretty damn hot that day, so I was sitting in the shade behind the park's tennis court, leaning up against a tree.

I was sitting in my own little world with my legs under me, the plastic baggie in my lap. I sat forward a little and arched my back, trying to work my fingers into my pants pocket to get my bowl.

"There you are, Wesley Pipes," I said to my clear pink-swirled glass pipe. They sell them for tobacco use only, but everyone knows they're for weed. "Are you ready to go to work, mister?"

Talking to inanimate objects is never a good sign, but I was okay as long as the objects didn't talk back.

An almost imperceptible flicker caused me to turn my head … nothing. There were two sets of couples on the tennis courts. I sat absolutely still, searching, wholly alert, as I cupped the bowl and had my baggie perfectly hidden under my ass. I looked around. A chubby guy with a stained t-shirt sat on a park bench while a couple of little girls with matching blonde pigtails were swinging as their mothers chatted to each other with an occasional glance in their direction.

Everything seemed normal enough.

I wiggled off my baggie and opened it up, pinched some of the recently bought marijuana, and put it in the bowl. I fingered my lighter out of my pocket and lit it with an inhale.

I was in mid-exhale when something smacked my ponytail. I jumped, hitting my elbow against the tree bark, dropped my bowl, and scattered all of the baggies' contents throughout the grass.

"What the hell?" My voice cracked on the last word. I couldn't help it. I was startled.

I heard his laugh before I saw him. Chan Cooper came out from behind a tree he was using as a cover to hide from me. "You always scare this easy?"

"You chipped it," I said as I raised my bowl.

Sitting down beside me, he said, "Salem, you've been working with me for a couple of months now, right?"

My initial response of annoyance at being disturbed while having a deep and meaningful conversation with Wesley Pipes was being replaced with guarded interest.

"Yeah, but me working there doesn't fix this chip." I pointed at the barely noticeable chip in the bowl's glass, trying my best to change the subject or get him to make his point.

"I'll get you a new one," he said, "on our date."

"Date?"

"Yeah, I mean, if you want to." The way his brown eyes looked down then up in that embarrassed school-boy way was adorable.

"You think you got cool moves, Mr. Scruff?" I said with a smile. He gave a smile that rivaled mine, a lot whiter and a hell of a lot straighter. Scratching his small beard, "I try," he said.

"Well, breaking a girl's bowl is like breaking a girl's heart. So, I'm finding one that's *really* expensive."

"I'll even buy you more stuff to go with it." His head nodded toward the now nearly empty baggie.

"All right, you got a date."

"Cool," he said as he got up. "Don't be late to work."

"I still got a few hours to waste," I said as I watched his brown curls bounce while he walked away.

I couldn't help myself, but when he was out of earshot, I laughed. I couldn't decide whether or not that was one of the coolest or one of the *lamest* ways I've seen a guy pick up a girl.

I shifted my fingers in the grass to see if any of my scattered pot could be salvaged, but unfortunately, that was a lost cause. It's very hard to pick grass out of grass if you know what I mean.

I got up and wiped my hands on my jeans. After putting my lighter up, I took out my cell phone to check the time.

Oh shit!

I didn't have a few hours until work, I only had a few minutes. I was going to be late.

I started toward the Casanova Theater at a jog. I fully understood the pot-heads' terminology of 'one-toker,' but just in case I needed clarification on its definition, it hit me all at once. I was a little dizzy; my mouth was already going dry, and I was starting to hear the wha-wha sound.

To my ears, and more than likely only my ears, my footfalls on the sidewalk were sounding like the beat of a song. I was trying my best to count how many times my ponytail bounced off my back, but before too long, I was at the doors of the theater.

I stumbled slightly but caught myself by grasping the door handle for balance, preventing a fall. My misfortune didn't stop there but merely started. Unforeseen by my drug-addled brain, I caught hold of the door, that is true, but the damn door pushed open. With the door opening with my weight, my feet slipped, and then I fell forward. "Fuck!" I cried out through clenched teeth after giving the metal door frame a violent kiss. I moaned my discomfort through my palm, trying my best not to draw attention.

I was in the theater; nevertheless, mouth pain or not ... I managed to show up on time. As I made my way inside further, nearing the snack bar, I heard John and Chan talking about zombie movies and how George Romero was the rightful owner and creator of all things 'zombie.'

"Hey," Matty interrupted them as I approached. "Every zombie movie is the same; how can y'all watch them like that? I mean, they all have the hero, the stuck-up bitch, the asshole, and the one-and-only-guy-who-knows-what's-happening. The hot chick always lives or dies last, and we cheer when the douchebag gets eaten. It's so repetitive."

"And what would you suggest?" John asked sarcastically.

"That's easy." Matty gave a shrug and eye-roll, "*Fifty Shades of Gray*, of course."

"Oh, please." John blurted out.

"Give me a break." Chan waved her comment off like a stubborn gnat. "What?" Matty defended, "It's a touching movie."

"Touching what? Your G-spot?" I added my first line in this conversation with drug-induced humor.

"That is the most important," Matty said frankly, starting her inventory of candy bars.

"I give up." Chan said and began to walk away, but not before adding, "See me later?"

I nodded my head, and as Chan and John left, Matty stopped what she was doing.

"What was *that*?"

"What was *what*?"

"Bitch," Matty gave a knowing smile, "spill it. I want details."

"What details?" I teased. After waiting long enough to annoy her, I said, "he asked me out on a date."

"You said yes?" She gave a mock gagging sound.

"Eww, that beard makes him look 35 instead of 25."

"I think he looks good."

"Eww."

"Well, okay then Mrs. I-Know-What's Good Looking, what type of guys do you like?"

"I like boyish looks and-"

My drug-addled brain interrupted, "Oes it iggle en I ooo at?" I said while pushing my finger on my top row of teeth.

"What?"

I removed my finger. "Does it wiggle when I do that?"

"No, why-" she fixed her eyes on mine, then they went wide. "Are you high?"

"No, I don't do that. No," I was scared.

"Your eyes are like glass girl. It's okay; I get high, too."

"Really?"

"Yeah, my daily diet is one of Vicodins and Percocets."

"I don't do pills," I shook my head. "I only smoke a little pot."

"Good god, woman, calm down. I'm not the

five-o," she placed her hand on mine. "I'm not trying to be your human Pez dispenser. But if you ever want one, just ask, okay?"

"Yeah, thanks." I took a sip of the soda and then left her to sell popcorn. I took the hall on the right that led to the screen room. A door on the left gave way to a staircase, which went up to the projection booths' door. The door has a faded sign that meant to say STAFF ONLY, but a few of the letters have worn off so badly that, at first glance, the sign says STANLY.

For some reason only known to stoners, I found the sign extremely fun tonight. I had to bite my tongue to prevent laughing. Steve Hodges, my boss, was in the booth preparing the reel-to-reel to be switched after showing a Popeye cartoon. Hodges tried his best to run the theater like it was in the 50s, which meant showing a short cartoon before the film and showing only classic movies. To him, the classic stopped in 1994 after *Forrest Gump* and *Pulp Fiction*.

I glanced at the cartoon and had to bite my tongue again. I was aware that very soon, this trick would cease to work; soon, it was going to laugh or die.

"There you are," Steven glanced from the projector.

"Thought I'd show the cartoon, then leave it to

ya."

"Thanks." I managed to say.

"No prob." He switched out the cartoon for the movie in no time at all. I hoped I could become as quick as he was, but I was still learning. As the opening credits of *See No Evil, Hear No Evil* rolled on the screen, the third of four movies Pryor and Wilder made together, he headed for the door. When the door shut behind him, I pressed my mouth to my cupped hand and laughed as quietly as I could. I laughed until tears sprang from my eyes. When the fit (and that was what it really felt like, a kind of stoner seizure) had passed, I looked toward the door with attentive, curious, slightly teary eyes, hoping that I had been quiet enough to pass under the radar of Steve Hodges.

The coast was clear.

I giggled again when I let out a little fart.

It was just so loud in this room, great acoustics.

I took my drink and sat down at the projector, the familiar sound of the film reel spinning filling the room. I took a sip of the ice-cold drink, almost moaning as I felt it tickling my throat as I settled in for the movie. The dimly lit room and the soft glow of the screen from the cutout square created a cozy atmosphere.

Now, this was relaxing.

As the movie reached its halfway point, a sense of unease creeped in. The excitement of the film was starting to fade and my thoughts began to drift to the upcoming date I had planned for tonight. Was this really what I wanted? Was I ready for this next step in my life?

I took another sip, the cool liquid soothing my nerves as I tried to push aside my doubts. I was looking forward to this date, wasn't I? Right? What if it didn't go well? What if I wasn't ready for a relationship?

After work, I went straight home and set up a movie as I always do. Halfway through the film, I was jolted from the attention I was giving it. My phone lit up with a new text, and Wednesday's roof-top cello pieces jerked me away from the stoplight just for a moment.

A little over an hour later, I was as downtown as Petula Clark, pulling down Matty's friends' street with its old gray flower-child tenement buildings and rusting fences and garbage bags piled high at the curbs of every other house. The street looked like a dilapidated chunk of upper-state blight plopped down beside the countryside.

She was waiting on the sidewalk, a few houses up from her friend's crib. The place she used as her cover was probably the worst on the whole street. It looked like more of a wood-shingled shack than a house with a rusting shell of a Cadillac under its listing carport.

She opened the car door and sat down. "Please tell me you got a cigarette. All I got is my pop's vape, and if I wanted to suck that hard on something with no pleasure … I would just go get a guy on the side."

I pulled out a pack of cigarettes and gave her one, "There ya go, you can stop feenin'."

"Thanks a ton. I was turning into Jodeci there for a sec."

"You stupid Matty," I laughed.

"Thanks for picking me up from here."

"No problem. I wasn't doing a hell of a lot anyway." We drove for a little while, chit-chatted, and chain-smoked my pack of cigarettes until it was empty. I ran the car in circles, trying to find this place while I was high. Finally, I managed to find it and dropped her off.

"Be careful, Matty."

"You too. See ya at work. Thanks again."

After seeing her go inside, I pulled off and headed to my place.

Now, sitting on my couch, I wondered where the hell all my weed went. I guess I'll have to hit up Amy on that offer to crash for a while at her place. I grabbed my phone and sent her a quick text and inquired about a small bag. She responded almost immediately with open arms to her crib. I gathered my things and headed toward her apartment.

I was feeling the need to cut the edge off a little. I was stressing about work, the temptation of Matty's offer, and my upcoming date I was still unsure of. I was stressing over life in general. Here I was at my age, still not sure what the hell I wanted out of life or what made me happy.

I just needed some weed.

I made my way to Amy's place in little to no time. Once there, she quickly answered the door with a smile.

She stood by the door with her arms folded, facing me, hips cocked to one side. She had white hair now. Not white-blonde, not platinum-blonde, but snow white, white as marble, bound up like a captured cloud to bare the lines in her slender throat.

"You like? After watching Enid Sinclair's wonderful hair colors, I was inspired to try this out."

"Yeah, I do.", I said, noticing I was looking at her a little closer than usual. Man, I need a buzz to help clear up my thoughts.

"Well, come on in!"

I followed her inside and made myself at home on her couch. I dropped my phone and my cigarettes on the coffee table and sat back. "So, what kind we working with tonight?"

"I got some hydro I've been saving for us, and I got some really good mid-grade for you if you still want that dime," she answered from the kitchen. She came into the living room holding two cans of soda. As she took her place on the couch, she handed one to me.

"Thanks"

"No problem."

We fell into the groove of things. She wrapped a dime up in a baggie. I packed the pipe for the two of us, and she grabbed the remote for the TV. We smoked and passed the pipe around watching *Friday the 13th, Part VII: The NewBlood.*

Or, better known to me as a terrible attempt to make a *Jason vs Carrie* that failed. After we finished the movie and were halfway through the next, I was pretty much done for the day and decided to head back to my own apartment. Had to get out of there before I was too baked to walk or before I took a hit like Walberg had in *Ted 2* when he couldn't find his way home.

TATTERED

4

Breathe easy.

As I look back at these times in my life I can't help but think of the old cliche, 'If I had known then what I know now.' How those words echo on and on inside my mind like a rubber ball bouncing down an endless staircase. As if the words possess a life of their own, which, I suppose they do now. I have to read just myself in this chair; it's getting a little uncomfortable. As I say these words, my hands shake, and my breathing is almost nonexistent. My eyes burn from trying my damndest to stop the tears, wanting so desperately to fall.

Sorry, where was I? Oh, yeah. I was… *My head is throbbing, my stomach is queasy, and I want nothing more than to stop telling you this.*

But I have to.

I was…

Breathe easy.

Just…

breathe easy.

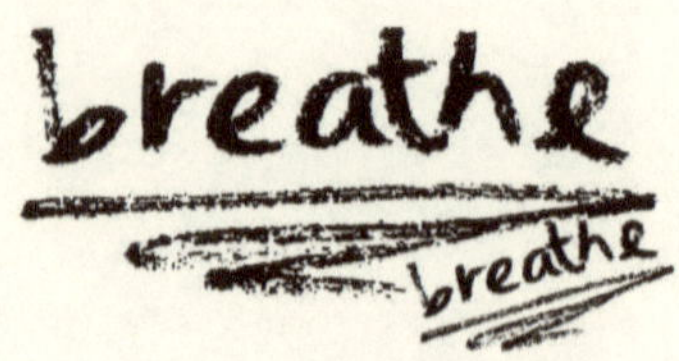

What the hell is wrong with me?

Here I am on a pretty good date with a hot guy. He'd picked me up at my apartment, bought me a new bowl (not to mention a small dime bag), and took me to one of the best Mexican restaurants in town (Burrito Brothers). Yet, I felt out of place and somewhat uncomfortable with his attempts to come off as sexy.

"So, he began, "wanna play a game?"

I laughed. "What is this *Saw,* or are you Chucky now?"

"Nah, seriously, I want to get to know ya a little better," he said. "You like scary movies? What's your favorite scary movie?"

I had to fight back another laugh, "Really? If I say it's *Scream,* will the questions stop?"

"I'm just trying to find some common ground."

"As long as it's not Ludlow's burial ground."

"What?"

"Nothing, never mind."

We were driving past Putt-Putt Palace near the roller skating rink when he looked over, "Want to make a pit stop at a quiet place?"

"Goodness, Evelyn, can the movie references be any easier?"

"What? I'm just looking for a place to talk is all. You wanna talk?"

I think I was old enough to know that people who started off any answer with 'just what to talk' were apt to go on by telling you straight-faced, that money grew on trees, girls didn't fart, and Elvis was still alive and currently living in Vegas.

"Really?" I tried my best to hide my doubts.

"Yeah, really," Chan's voice suggested my doubt was obvious. "Salem, I'm not that type of guy. Come on."

"Sorry, I don't mean to offend your character." I tried to put on a decent smile.

"You want to?"

"Sure, but no funny stuff."

"Scouts Honor." His smile was heard as well as seen.

We drove a little further before he pulled into an empty lot and parked behind a closed store.

"A little radio?" He asked as he fiddled with the knobs, found an okay station, and turned it low enough to be heard but not distracting. Chan then turned in his seat a little and tried to pull off the all but too-familiar Mr. Cool move by acting like he was stretching and put his arm over my seat.

I tried to put a smile in my words, "So what ya got on your mind? Besides putting your arm around me, that is."

He glanced at his arm as if he hadn't noticed he moved it, then he gave a small grin and began to lean forward.

I let him kiss me, but when he tried to part my lips with his tongue, I put my hand on his chest and gently pushed him away. "What's wrong?"

"Nothing, it's just weird."

"Hey, I'm not weird." He smirked, "I'm limited edition." He leaned in again. A small smile appeared, but left quickly. "It's not you, it's me." I gently pushed his chest again.

"Yeah, right." These words were followed by an

eye-roll and another attempt to lean in.

"No, seriously," I was a little defensive now. "It just doesn't feel right. I'm sorry." I pushed harder this time.

"Sorry?" His tone was pure sarcasm, "You mean I spent like a hundred bucks tonight and can't even get a kiss."

"Chan, I'm not a whore!"

"I'm not calling you a whore!"

"Just take me home." I shifted in my seat and faced the window.

He scoffed. "No need for attitude, Salem."

"Home." I demanded, but then said, "Please."

He did as I asked and wasted no time leaving. I'd barely closed the car door before he pulled away.

I walked the short path to my door, fumbled with my keys, and dropped them twice before I made it into my apartment.

Putting my purse on the coffee table, I turned the lamp on and sat on the couch.

What the fuck was all that about?

I asked myself this question in an assortment of ways, but no matter the words I used, it all boiled down to the same.

What the fuck was that all about?

I even thought the first thing men tried to use was a woman's excuse, but my period was last week and was never that bad to begin with. I turned the small box fan by the couch on and then got out my new bowl. I needed to clear my head and do some thinking.

I got the bowl packed and ready and repeatedly tried to light it with an obviously dead lighter. To say I was getting agitated would be like saying Gandhi looked hungry. I finally gave up and got another one out of my purse.

Blowing out the smoke, I asked myself the same question again– but still didn't have an answer.

After watching *The High Note* for the fourth time in my life, I started channel surfing. I stopped when I saw Liv Tyler and Scott Speedman get an unexpected knock on their door from three masked strangers.

I picked up my cell and decided to text Matty:

I started tearing up little pieces of bud apart to get another bowl-pack ready when I got her reply:

I looked at my pile of pot I was fingering, not much, but I could afford to share, and it might help me forget about my date:

I laughed at her response and started collecting my paraphernalia. Bowl, check. Pot, check. Lighter, check. All the tools needed to be a successful stoner. After fumbling to find the right one, I put the key in the ignition but didn't turn it. I briefly considered just staying home. I looked through the windshield and thought of the night thus far, and I had to admit it's been pretty shitty. I decided to drive the long way.

As I drove, I rolled the window down so the cool air would help clear my mind. It was a clear night. Ahead of me, country roads curved and wound through beautiful trees—finally, the lights of the city limits cut through the darkest of the country.

I was at Matty's house in less than fifteen minutes. I noticed again it was a normal looking one-story story with a patchy lawn and a trampoline and swing set in the backyard. The one house on the left was abandoned and boarded. On the right, the owners had a nice chain-link fence and bars over their windows. She must've heard my car door closing because she opened the door as I climbed the stairs to the front porch. She looked exhausted, her hair pushed back with a headband.

"Come on in," she held the door for me. "I've been trying to braid Lisbeth's hair. Ugh! Even with YouTube, I can't figure it out."

"Guess you can cross hairstylist off career choices, huh?" I smiled.

"Give me those," I pulled at one of the many hair ties she had on her wrist. "I'll do it."

"You sure? Guess I'll be a beauty school drop-out."

"No graduation day for you," I said in a sing-song voice. In the living room, a little girl sat watching the TV intently from a couch that looked like it might have been new in 1970. She sang along with a song that was playing. She had long, straight, stop-sign red hair and, surprisingly, no freckles.

"This is Lisbeth," Matty said, patting her head, which the little girl waved off and pointed at the movie.

"Is this *Pitch Perfect*?"

"Yes," Matty sighed. "She's been watching it like every other day since she got it…like a month ago. Last time, it was *Hedwig and the Angry Inch* until I told her I couldn't do any more of the freak-show dragulas."

"Don't got the others?"

"Oh, God, yes," she clasped her hands in mock prayer, "no more, please, don't make anymore."

I sat on the couch beside Lisbeth. Matty gave me all the hair ties and told her sister I was here to save the night with my salon expertise.

"Thank you," Lisbeth said politely, then sat on the floor between my legs. I was having fun. I wasn't thinking about my shitty date or the other strange thoughts I was having. I sat enjoying the movie and even caught myself humming along with Anna Kendrick and Brittany Snow in the shower.

"All done," I ran my fingers along the braids as if they were wind chimes.

"That's our cue," Matty said, nodding her head to the side and waving for me to follow.

I followed her down the hall, passing a wall of pictures and a small table holding a brown leaf plant I assumed was dead. We stepped over an overflowing laundry basket and went to the back porch. My bowl was ready in record time, and we began smoking. Inhale, wait while the other took their hit, exhale, repeat.

Matty reached into the neck of her shirt and into the cup of her bra, pulling out three tiny pills in plastic wrapping.

"Want one?"

"Nah, I'm good," I took another toke from my bowl.

"So, how was the date?" she nudged my elbow with hers.

I laughed, "Oh, that … 'bout as fun as a sandpaper dildo."

"That fun, huh?" she chuckled, then coughed out a lung full of smoke. We finished the bowl, and I even smoked one of her cigarettes; the night now not a complete loss. It was saved by a little friendly companionship, not to mention she wasn't trying to force-feed me her tongue down my throat. "Guess I better get going," I said reluctantly, not wanting to go home to face my own thoughts again but knowing I had to eventually.

"Alright. Be safe and buckle up," she laughed.

Back at my place, before I threw a blanket over myself, I thought again about what happened during my date, and once again, I thought the same thing. What the fuck was all that about?

5

Breathe easy.

I can do this.

I can do this.

This is where all the memories start skittering through my head, like disconnected images from old movies.

This is the part that hurts the most.

My mouth is really dry. Can I have some water?

Thank you.

I wipe away the tear that was running down my cheek before I begin again. ***Breathe easy.***

The next day's sky was blanketed in big fluffy clouds that floated along in its neverending vastness, the kind that looked more like spring than mid-fall. I made my way down the cracked sidewalk trying my best to think of tonight's presentation of *Ferris Bueller's Day Off* and how no matter what movie Jennifer Gray was in– I would think of *Dirty Dancing* first.

Last night kept creeping in like a persistent and after spilled sugar. Birds chirruped in the trees, sharing the previous night's secrets and plans for the day (maybe even what type of car to poop on). A few leaves in this part of town were just beginning to turn. They drifted and skittered across the street. The way some made it all the way across without getting hit by a car made me think of the movie Rip Torn, where his character said, 'If you can dodge traffic, you can dodgeball.'

My stress level was slowly rising like a thermometer. I didn't want Chan to hate me for two reasons: One, he was a nice guy. Two, he works where I work. I didn't want my job to become awkward and have to duck and dodge every time we got close to each other.

I would've had a talk with Wesley Pipes this afternoon, but I smoked all of my pot last night trying to find an answer to the question that still remained elusive. Finally, at the theater, my job, for the most part, consumed my thoughts.

I raised my hand to John as I neared the ticket booth. "Hey."

"Hello there," he tried a bad Christopher Walken impersonation.

"Think Steve's ever going to hire someone to take tickets?"

"Maybe he's talking to someone now."

"Really? Hope they're better than the last one."

"Oh, one-day-wonder," he laughed, "tickets just weren't his thing." I agreed and made my way inside.

Matty was behind the snack bar with her elbows on the counter, face in her hands, and her eyes closed.

"Nodding off are we?"

"Salem, it's called a horizontal life pause." She reached under the counter, grabbed a Coke, and placed it in front of me, all with eyes still closed. "Thanks."

Her response could've been 'Sure' or even 'Anytime,' but it came out only as a grunt.

"Talk with you later, alligator."

She gave another guttural response. I had a feeling it could've been 'You're lame,' though.

As I got to the door leading to the projector, I

heard laughter. Opening the door, I saw Chan and a girl I'd never seen before coming down the stairs. "Hey there, Salem, '' Chan said. I guess last night was forgotten by the looks of his smile, "Just showing our newest employee around." "What's up," said the girl, who reminded me of a Barbie doll; she had such flawless skin. Her hair was these dark, bouncy curls. "My name's Lily."

"Well, nothing much, Lily."

"Good to meet you, Salem."

"Uh-uh," I made my way up as they went down.

My first thought was how long would it be before Chan tried out some of his moves on her. Was I jealous? We just had a date last night, and even though we had an argument, it wasn't all bad. One day later and already, he was undressing another girl with his eyes. Maybe I was just upset about that.

I sat my soda down a safe distance from the equipment. Tonight, Hodges allowed me to pick the short skit. I fed the film into the projector and had a Tom and Jerry cartoon rolling in a short burst of practiced hand movements. I was hoping before too long Hodges might allow me to choose the feature film as well as the cartoon. I had my eyes wide *open* for Stanley Kubrick's

Eyes Wide Shut.

With approximately two-thirds of my soda gone (and twenty minutes of the film), I heard a knock on the door. I've become accustomed to Hodges coming at odd times to check on how I was doing or asking if I need a break (the latter was asked more so during our double or triple features).

"I was told to give you this." The new girl handed me another Coca-Cola.

"Thanks."

"Hodges was busy fixing some kind of cash register malfunction," she said with a smile. "By the looks of it, it was more of a cashier malfunction." She quietly pulled a chair from the back wall that had been propped next to the reel-to-reel case racks that held God only knows how many movies. "Do you care if I watch from here?"

I motioned for her to sit and placed my finger to my lips in the universal sign of 'shut up.'

"Oh, yeah, sorry," she whispered. "I like this movie, but she always makes me think of Dirty Dancing."

A long silence was shared between us as I took sips of my soda. The seconds counted by the steady click-hum of the projector.

"So," my nerves a little stronger now, "you into Chan?" The question probably came out bitchy, but I was curious.

Her lips twitched upward to begin a smile. "He's not my type."

"Oh."

"You like him, don't you?"

"No, not really." Now that I had a chance to vent, I took advantage of it, even though she was a complete stranger. Somehow, it felt good to just let it out. "We went out last night, but…" I couldn't think of any other way to put it. "It just felt wrong."

"What was wrong?" Was that concern I heard in her voice?

"I'm not sure," I was being honest. "We had a good time, and then he tried to kiss me and it felt wrong. So I told him so. "We got into a little argument, and he took me home."

"Was it the kiss that felt wrong?"

"No, not really. It was really the whole thing."

"So, it didn't feel like a date?"

"Not really. Well, his come-ons kept reminding me, but it still felt more like just friends hanging out."

"I understand."

"Really?" Maybe she had the answer to my question.

Suddenly, she burst out laughing. "Sorry, that just cracks me up," she said, nodding toward the movie with another fit of giggles.

I gave a crooked smile of amusement. Looking at her, I noticed she wasn't beautiful like a model but genuinely attractive. Her skin was dark and reminded me of chocolate. Then I felt like an ass for thinking of her complexion as a stereotypical description of a Black woman, but her being here was very liberating regardless of my thoughts at the moment.

I would've hated to be up here all night alone.

She got up from her seat and picked up her soda can. "I gotta go. I'm leaving the scene, jellybean."

I gave an unexpected laugh. "Alright. Talk with you later, Lily."

"Yeah," she smiled. "See ya, Salem."

"See ya."

I watched her leave before turning back to give the film my attention. Even though my eyes were on the movie, I was mentally replaying my conversation with Lily. I barely even knew this girl, and yet I was opening up to her. Why? I guess because she just gave off an aura of comfort that put my mind at ease. I still wondered why.

My mind was going in circles, reminding me of those beautiful old-time carousels with prancing steeds and racing stallions. I could visualize the flashing lights and the steamy calliope music. The ride was over, and so was the movie.

I took the reel-to-reel tape and put it back in its tin case, shelved it in the right place, and then dusted the equipment off before heading toward the door. Finally, downstairs in the lobby, I saw Matty was wiping down the glass display top.

"How's it goin'?" I said.

"Alright, I guess. Given the fact that my mom took my phone, my sister scratched one of my favorite movies, and my period reminds me of the walls of Amityville Horror."

"Eww, too much info."

She just laughed.

"So, you like the new girl? I saw her go up to the booth."

"I don't know. Didn't talk much, just asked questions," I said, not wanting to say how I felt at ease with her.

"Want some of the leftover popcorn?"

"Why not," I said, accepting a small bag.

"What are you getting into tonight?"

"I'm going home and crash. I'm tired. You?"

"Probably meet up with this biker gang and have them run a train on me." Her face showed complete seriousness for all of two seconds before a fit of laughter exploded from her. "Just kidding."

"Oh, man, I was gonna come with you." I threw a piece of popcorn at her. "Maybe next time."

"Did you fix your cash register?"

"Yep, the drawer got stuck."

"Thanks for the Coke."

"The one I gave to you before you went up?" She looked at me with eyebrows raised. "You already said as much for that one."

I let the subject go. "Well, I got a question."

"Okay. Is it serious?"

"Nah, not really."

She pretended to wipe her forehead. "Whoo. I almost gave a fuck. Scared the shit out of myself."

"Oh, really? That how you feel?" I threw a piece of popcorn at her.

"Spill," she said with a grin.

I cleared my throat. "I'm dry. Do you know where to get some pot?"

She turned her head left, then right, then back at me. "You the police?" she laughed. "Nah, grass ain't my thing. But I can give ya something to get ya by until tomorrow if you want."

"I only smoke a little weed, Matty."

"I know, but this is a downer, so it'll kinda be the same high."

"Really?"

"Yeah, trust me." She grabbed her purse from under the counter and was already unzipping it before I could respond.

"Okay, but only this once," I felt the need to add.

On my way back to my apartment, the pills seemed to burn a hole in my pocket. I found myself touching the pocket where I put them every other block I drove. My skin seemed woven through with copper wires carrying a low electrical charge. I was distantly aware that the hairs on the nape of my neck were standing as erect as porcupine quills. I knew from television that painkillers seemed to be the most popular form of drug use, and I was a little eager to find out why now that I had some.

I made a little vow to myself: no matter the quality of the high, this was going to be a one-time thing. I was only doing it now because my pot dealer was out until tomorrow.

Anyway, you can't get hooked using one time.

Could you?

I didn't let my anxiousness get the best of me, though. Instead, my mind was put at ease just by my keys sliding into the key slot of my front door and closing it behind me. My anticipation was put on hold as I turned on the lights in my living room, turned on the boob tube, and placed my purse on the coffee table.

Tim Curry's voice seemed to follow me into the kitchen as he yelled commands to catch the kid who wasn't supposed to be in the hotel. I opened my refrigerator to grab a soda that wasn't there and made a mental note to go pick some up tomorrow.

Mildly frustrated, I drank a glass of water and refilled it to take with me, but then decided on a shower and poured the water out.

Before heading to the shower, I remembered the pills. Taking them out of my jeans, I placed them next to my purse.

The shower was soothing, as always. There was really nothing better than a hot shower to wash away the day's troubles (not to mention the stink). Twenty minutes later, I was padding my way back to the kitchen barefoot and wearing nothing but a pair of panties and an old Alicia Keys t-shirt that hung down and brushed my knees. I got a glass of water and went back to the living room. As I sat the glass down, my eyes went instantly to the pills.

There were two of them, not much bigger than a breath mint each. As I fingered one of them, I asked myself, do I want to do this? I put one in my mouth and took it with a shot of water.

I repeated the action with the other rounded mass of intended medication. Then I waited.

And I waited.

After waiting long enough and getting bored, I decided to go to bed. The pills weren't working anyway, so I might as well go to sleep. I rose from the couch, but my legs turned to rubber before I could get to a standing position. I wobbled, my legs shook unsteadily, and then I fell back on the couch. I lowered my head until it almost touched my knees, closed my eyes, and took a long, deep breath, then another. I lifted my head and felt like I was swimming. I didn't exactly faint, but had started to pull away from the world. I was looking through a dirty camera lens rather than something I was actually in, it seemed. Everything came in and out of focus. I fell back onto the couch, amazed by the feelings coming to meet me.

This was a feeling I'd never had before.

It was all so intense. I knew at that moment my vow would be broken.

TATTERED

6

"Breathe easy."

I swallowed hard, and it seemed to echo in the silence. The quiet felt suffocating. I ran a hand up my left cheek and stared stupidly at the flakes of dried blood in my palm. I explored a little more in my nervous calm-me-down rubbing and felt scratches on my arms.

My guts ached, and my face hurt. My stomach was slowly becoming a lead ball that seemed to be expanding until it filled me from head to toe. "Hurt me with the truth, but never comfort me with a lie." That was one of my father's favorite sayings. I also found that telling the truth not only hurts but can slowly pick you apart and leave you tattered.

Tears came, great racking sobs that made my ribs hurt. I closed my eyes, and all these memories were there as though engraved on the back of my eyelids. I'm sorry for crying.

Thank you.

I used the tissue to dab at my eyes before I began again.

"Breathe easy."

The next day at the theater, we all had to show up early to prepare for the triple feature. We were having a mini Bogart-fest showing Humphrey's classics: Casablanca, Key Largo, and Brother Orchid.

I held a corner of the poster as Matty taped it in place.

"Ya know, you wouldn't have thought it, but Bergman was taller than Bogart. The difference was so much that in certain scenes, he had to have blocks on his shoes," I said.

"Uh," Matty acknowledged without a hint of really caring about the movie. She cut the final piece of tape from the roll and held it over where she intended to put it.

"Well, that does it," Matty said as she patted the last corner of the Casablanca movie poster we taped on the wall behind the cash register.

"Looks good, darlin'," Hodges complimented in a very bad Bogart fashion.

"Does it look good enough for a break?" Matty asked. "I'd like to go to the Quick-Stop for a few minutes to pick up a few things."

"Yeah, sure." Hodges looked at me and asked, "You going also?"

"If it's okay."

"Yeah, just don't stay too long. Alright, you two?"

"Alright," Matty and I said in unison.

"I'll be back." I tried my best, Arnold voice, but failed miserably. Matty grabbed her purse, and we left the theater and started walking to the gas station at the end of the street. The Quick-Stop was a family-run establishment that sold cheap off-brand drinks, snacks, microwavable pizzas, beer, and cigarettes. After a short walk, we were making our way through the parking lot. A huge sign welcomed us with the proclamation: Slushies Half Off.

"Oh, slushies," Matty said to no one in particular as we entered the store. The aisles were close together but easy to navigate. The shelves were packed, crammed, and stacked full of all types of low-quality convenience store crap. As I searched for a flavor of chips that would meet the requirements of small snack hunger, I also contemplated whether or not I should buy one of the single cigarettes they sold for fifty cents and decided not to. It was bad enough that I smoked pot, so I'd let my lungs have at least a small break and not irritate them with the fumes of tobacco right now.

Matty came back from the slushy machine, announcing between sips, "They have the Cheerwine kind."

"Ya know, you're supposed to wait until you buy it before you drink it."

She just smiled and said, "For them to expect that when it's a self-serve is as useless as the 'g' in lasagna because it's gonna happen." I grabbed a bag of nacho cheese curls and followed her to the counter, pulled an orange soda from the cooler of ice, and placed my items next to hers.

"I got it," I told her, hoping to win a few points for the question I was going to ask her. I always hated to ask for favors, even when I knew I wouldn't be in debt long.

"Dat be four-fifty," the cashier said as I rummaged

through my purse to find my wallet.

"Ya sure?" asked Matty.

"It's fine," I handed a five-dollar bill across the counter and got fifty cents worth of dimes and nickels back.

We were heading out the door as I twisted the top off my bottle and repositioned my purse strap. I let Matty take a few more sips of her slushy before I popped the question.

"So, umm...do you have any more of those pills?"

The straw fell out of her mouth as her lips turned into a smile. "Ya liked it, huh?"

"Yeah."

"I knew ya would," she smiled. "Hey, follow me to the bathroom."

"Alright. So you got some."

"Just follow me."

And that's exactly what I planned to do.

We walked across Liberty Street onto Sunset Avenue. Even though it was a little chilly, several of the stores had their front doors open; signs sat out on the sidewalk, welcoming people to come in and look around.

A card table was out front of The Bookworm covered in pamphlets and flyers. A short woman with a contagious smile and small blue-frame glasses offered us each a flier as we walked by.

"It'd be nice to see you there," she said as we took the flier she offered. I folded the piece of paper and shoved it into my purse. Matty glanced at it, then made a snowball out of it and threw it in the next trash can she passed.

"It's a gathering of gays," she let out with an eye roll.

After a few more minutes of walking, the Casanova doors were closing behind us, and we were down the hall and in the bathroom. I've never liked public restrooms. I just believe a bathroom is too personal a place to share, especially by girls. A fact that most will refute as false: women tend to be a lot nastier when using public restrooms. They are full of hair and scabs and snot and signs of heavy flows when bloody tampons are left in the trash can, but I do have to admit the Casanova bathrooms are pretty damn clean.

Matty was searching thoroughly through her purse. "Now, not many people know this, but I'm the happiness fairy." She pulled out a cupped hand and placed it on the sink counter. "Now, I bring Happy Pills for you. Now smile, dammit! This shit's expensive." She uncurled her fingers to reveal four pills.

"How much?"

"I'll cut ya a deal. Two for twenty, that's ten cheaper than I paid."

"Wow. That's pretty steep."

"Told ya, this shit can be expensive."

"Okay. Deal." I rifled through my cash and found two tens, thinking the high was worth the price.

"Now, I'm not a dealer, so if ya want me to, I can meet you up with mine next time I go."

"Yeah, sure. When will that be?" One pill is already going down my throat.

"Tomorrow, probably."

"Okay, that's cool." The other pill is pocketed for later consumption. I checked my phone for the time.

"Guess it's almost showtime."

"Well, let's get to work."

"Hasta la vista, baby."

Nearly two hours had passed. I had my hair tied back in a ponytail and my feet kicked up on one of the broken chairs, watching the movie and occasionally repeating a quote from the film.

"Round up the usual suspects," I whispered to myself. The effects of the pill I'd taken about fifteen minutes ago were starting to kick in, so I gave a small giggle I would have let pass if I had been sober.

The sound of the door closing caused me to look behind me and see the source of the noise. It was only Lily, so instead of trying to sit properly, I kept my feet up. She was holding two bottles of Coke.

As she sat down, I noticed her hair for the first time today. She had been working with John and getting used to how the ticket sales were done. "Wow?"

She only smiled and flicked her braids out of her eyes with a quick movement of her head, adjusted herself, and then handed me one of the sodas. "I was told to give you this," she said, then added the question, "You like these?"

I gave it a brief study. The braids were small; there were what looked like hundreds of them, reaching the bottom of her jawline. "You pull it off pretty good." I cracked open my soda and took a sip, "Here's looking at you, kid."

She smiled. "Louis, I think this is the beginning

of a beautiful friendship."

I laughed, took another sip, then said, "So, you've seen this before."

"Oh yeah. It's a classic."

"So, what did you do before catching this gig?"

"Well, before my grandfather died, I used to help him a lot. He did part-time landscaping. Mowing lawns, raking leaves, planting flowers and bushes, sometimes trees."

"Pretty cool."

"In the winter, I sometimes shoveled out driveways."

"And this was where?"

"Monroe. I lived with my grandparents, which is also why I've seen this movie," she smiled. "What about you?"

"No one to speak of, really, just me." I hate talking about my years growing up because it's just not much to speak on.

"We don't have to talk about it." I guess my discomfort was showing. I smiled weakly, grateful for her understanding. I put my feet on the floor, placed my soda on the now empty chair seat, and changed the subject. "Your hair does look good."

"Thanks," her lips twitched upward. "I like your outfit."

"Really?" I replied shyly and with doubt. I was wearing a pair of ripped jeans torn at one knee and a plain T-shirt.

"Yeah, it suits you."

"Thanks. You ever come here before working here?"

"Nah, what about you?"

"I came on a date a few years back. We watched the movie Bonnie and Clyde."

"That's a great one from the late sixties."

"Used to be one of my favorites," she took a small sip from her soda. "You know that Warren Beatty went out of his way to make the gunshots as loud as he could?"

"Learn something every day, huh?" I smiled.

"What's your favorite movie?"

"This week, you mean," I smiled. "I'm a big-time movie buff. I really love a lot, but the best I've seen lately… umm, oh, I watched Easy A the other day and—"

"Oh, I like that one. It's a fun movie."

"Yeah, Emma Stone is a good actress. Ever seen Zombieland?"

"Of course, Woody Harrelson is like one of the coolest guys ever."

"Oh my god! Finally, someone who agrees with me. He is so underrated."

"Isn't he, though? I've liked him ever since Natural Born Killers."

"Yes, that was just a mind fuck of a movie."

We shared a laughing fit as we did impersonations of Mallory Knox.

"Did you watch Key Largo?"

"Nah, I missed it helping John," she smiled. "Well, he was helping me, to be honest, with the ticket machine. I just couldn't get it to work."

"It's good. I read somewhere that Edward G. Robinson fought for leading man during trailers and poster designs and stuff. For example, the poster has Bogart's name first, which is usually the lead role, but Edward has the biggest picture and more centered, which is also usually reserved for the lead."

"That's pretty cool. I think the same thing happened with Clint Eastwood and Burt Reynolds in that... umm—"

"City Heat."

We chatted and laughed for a little while longer before we settled into mutual silence to watch the movie.

I reached for my drink, and my fingers brushed against her hand as she did the same. What felt like an electric spark ran down my arm, and our eyes met. Lily leaned in and touched her lips to mine briefly but drew back quickly. I was stunned, high, and confused.

"What the—"

"I'm sorry," Lily said while standing up and heading toward the door. "I'm sorry—" The door closing behind her cut off anything more.

She was gone.

Now, I was stunned, high, confused, and alone.

I was exhaling the toke I'd just taken from Wesley Pipes and wondering if I was sick in the head. I didn't mean the talking-to-yourself variety you see in old men feeding pigeons in the park where you know it's just old age's cruel joke, but the capital C crazy where I'd get hauled to the nuthouse in a straitjacket, shackles, maybe even a fucking mouthguard.

Nearly the entire quarter bag of weed was gone, and I still couldn't stop thinking about Lily's lips on mine.

I shouldn't.

It wasn't normal for a girl to kiss another girl.

It damn sure wasn't the typical reaction for the girl who got kissed by another girl to like it or enjoy it.

Did I enjoy it?

I dumped the bowl's ashes, pinched some more pot from the baggie, and began tearing it into little pieces. I packed the bowl, wiped my fingers on the leg of my jeans, and reached for the lighter. My fingertips pushed it further out of reach at first, so when I went to retrieve it, my eyes caught a glimpse of the folded flier playing peek-a-boo from my purse.

As I pulled the flier from its hiding place, I heard the famous line from "All About Eve" come from the television: "Fasten your seatbelts. It's going to be a bumpy night."

"Ain't that the truth," I muttered. I unfolded the flier. The top line said: "Attention LGBT Community of Asheboro."

The body of the flier discussed all the whats and whys of the meeting at apparently a different address than usual. The bottom gave reassurance that the meeting was a judgment-free, safe place, and completely confidential. The last word, "confidential," really grabbed my attention.

I scanned the page again and noticed the date and time. It was tonight, in another hour.

I still had my shoes on.

I was a little high, though... maybe more than a little, I admitted to myself. I grabbed my purse, flier still in hand, and headed out.

There was a small crowd going into the building. Some people were getting handshakes or shoulder pats. I even saw a couple of people getting hugs before going inside.

"Welcome." The flier lady shook my hand.

"Yeah, no problem."

"Would you like a name tag?" She had a marker and a name tag sticker.

"Yeah, sure. My name is Salem."

"Nice to meet you, Salem." She handed me my name tag. "My name is Denise. I'm the meeting facilitator, so any questions you have I'd be happy to answer."

"Don't you have to be gay for this?"

"No," she shook her head with a tiny smile, "these meetings are for everyone. Gay, bi, lesbian, trans, family members, friends, and straight allies of the LGBT community. They are for those seeking answers to their questions on sexuality and gender. To give and receive support. To hear positive messages in a judgment-free, safe, welcoming space. Even if you don't say a word, it's good you're here, Salem." She gave me a pat on the arm. "Please help yourself to any of the literature and snacks."

I walked in and breathed deeply, listened to the people already there, and tried to calm myself. My phone buzzed with a text, but I managed to ignore it. Reading the flier, I had envisioned a lonely crowd of crybabies dodging their real problems. I looked around the room. There were two tables. One covered in a small variety of drinks and snacks, the other stickers and booklets. Because of the pot, I ventured over gradually to the snacks despite feeling exposed.

I was stuffing my mouth with corn chips as a man walked over. He took a cup of some yellowish soda and said something that vaguely resembled, "What's your name?"

I took my hand out of the corn chip bag and pointed at my name tag; my mouth was still full, so I didn't want to be rude, but the gesture also seemed as such. He leaned in, almost close enough to see the color of my bra through my shirt as if visually impaired. I finally looked at him; other impairments were obvious. His outfit was a mismatched ensemble of frayed and stained khaki pants, a faded red shirt covered with lint, and a hat at least one size too big resting on his oversized ears. Unruly black hair crept from under the hat.

"Salem, nice to meet ya," he took a long swallow of his drink, "I'm Don." I lifted my hand still in the bag in a weak gesture of hello. I was still chewing as he left to sit in a chair, one of many that were placed in a circle in the center of the room.

I was getting cotton-mouthed, so I attempted to walk the few steps to beverages, swaying a little but caught my balance quickly.

The off-brand soda was one hell of a quencher for parched mouth; generic product or not, I emptied a cup in no time at all. My eyes were feeling heavy and kept wanting to drift closed, so I knew I was beginning to sober up.

I saw people were going toward the circle of chairs, but before heading in that direction, I downed another half cup of soda. In twenty minutes, I'll probably be fighting sleep and the need to piss.

I sat next to a handsome blond guy. He reached

up and fished his cell phone out of his breast pocket, tucked in behind a pack of cigarettes. His fingers started to pull the cigarettes out, to stomp them or chain-smoke them. I couldn't tell, but as he darted his eyes around the circle, he let go.

"Someday," he sighed, then punched a few keys on the phone before putting it back.

"Hello, everyone. I think we'll go ahead and start. Please remember this is a safe space. Share as little or as much as you wish. Welcome, everyone, my name is Denise. My preferred pronouns are she, her, and hers. I come to these meetings to offer my support."

The next to speak was a girl. She coughed and waved one hand past her face, fighting back tears, before she smiled, "My name is Charley. My pronouns are she, her, hers," she adjusted her skirt, "I'm here alone. Just looking for an ear and giving one."

She gestured to the man I already met to speak next.

"Hey, y'all. My name is Don. I'm here because of my husband, who passed a few months ago. He used to come to things like this, but I never went with him," he pinched the bridge of his nose, "I'm sorry."

"We're glad you're here, Don," said Denise.

"Thank you."

The middle-aged woman sitting next to him spoke next. She scratched her arm, the flannel sleeve wrinkled with the motion. "My name is Jamie. I answer to she, her, or just my name. Call me anything except late to lunch, umm... I'm currently in a relationship with an amazing woman. She should come with me next time, umm, I don't know, guess that's all for now." She looked at the guy next to her.

The blond guy's hand began to creep upward again before he realized it was his turn. "Oh, sorry. I'm Joey. I'm trying to stop smoking for my boyfriend, but I'm having some difficulties and thought coming may busy my mind some, so mainly I'm just here to listen, again, sorry."

After a beat of silence, I realized eyes were on me.

"My bad," I began, "Umm... My name is Salem umm... I... I really have no idea why I'm here, to be honest."

"Preferred pronouns?"

"Oh, yeah. She, her, hers, I guess. I don't really understand the need for that; shouldn't it be obvious?"

"No, it's not. We want to respect the individual and not make assumptions based on outward appearances. While someone may present or look to you as a female or male, their preferred pronouns may differ from what you and society think. We know, respect, and honor the truth that genitals do not define one's gender or gender expression, though much of the world would argue this," she paused to adjust her glasses, "it can be a very complex issue."

"Like me," added Charley, "look at me, what do you see?"

"A girl."

"Would you believe I was assigned male at birth?"

"No way."

Charley smiled and flipped her hair off her shoulder, exposing some wicked-looking inkwork.

As I sat there, my thoughts were elsewhere. Though I vaguely heard the conversations, I was too caught up in my own mind, so full of questions. I was surprised when Denise said the meeting was over and told us to feel free to stay and visit and to please eat the snacks.

As some wandered to the snack table and others said their goodbyes, I gathered my courage and went to talk to Denise.

"Could I talk to you?" I managed to say without stuttering.

"Of course," she nodded as a gesture to follow, and I did with gratitude of understanding.

"Salem, how was your first meeting?"

"Great... but I still have some questions that are bothering me."

"I think I know what your question will be."

"That obvious, huh?" I sighed shyly.

"No, no, just I've done this for a long time, honey. Do you think weightlifting is just for men?"

Her question caught me off guard, "No."

"Exactly, but there are a lot of people who do. I took last week off from the gym and went on some long walks. I'll go back next week and change it up a bit. My point is that people are complex, but society just wants to box, label, and force conformity of the masses. Different is a problem for many people."

"Guess that makes sense. I know a lesbian, but we're nothing alike, and I don't care for her coming on to me."

"The important thing here is who occupies your thoughts, who catches your eye, who do you imagine a relationship with, a future."

I swallowed. "It's a girl."

"Well, then, Salem, live and love your truth. It's

your life to live, not someone else's."

TATTERED

7

Breathe easy.

This feeling of being pushed by invisible hands into the part of the past I don't want to go is stronger now. I feel small…and vulnerable…and pissed off that I have to.

I know I have to.

I attempt to wipe my watery eyes but flinch from the touch. My head lowers, and my eyes drift to my lap. I choke back a sob.

I know I have to. Just give me a second, okay?

I look up and swallow.

Breathe easy…

breathe easy.

Beep beep. Beep beep.

I groan, hoping that it will go away.

Beep beep. Beep beep.

One more groan of annoyance escapes my lips.

BEEP! BEEP! BEEP!

Now, a desperate plea for more sleep and a deep moan indicative of my aggravation comes out of me.

BEEP! BEEP! BEE-

My hand slams on the alarm clock. "I'm up. Goddamn it, I'm up." The beeping is still persistent in spite of my groping hands. "Shut up. Please, shut up."Being nice didn't stop the alarm, so I did what my sleep-fogged mind told me to; I jerked the cord out of the socket.

"Thank you." I pressed my face deeper into my pillow, shifting my body to find a comfortable position, snuggled my blanket to my chin, and closed my eyes. I felt myself drift to that pleasant zone right before sleep.

Then my phone began to whistle the theme to *The Good, the Bad, and the Ugly,* alerting me that I had a new text message.

"I give up," I said, defeated. "I fucking give up." I kicked my blanket off my legs, rolled over on my back, picked an eye-booger out of each eye, and reached for my phone.

It was Matty:

> MATTY: Hey girl. I just got off, and by the way, I'm also getting off work soon. mtg with my guy in an hour, u coming?

I'd almost forgotten. Almost. It wouldn't have taken long, though, with a set of empty pockets and a baggie of nothing but the smell left in it.

My reply:

> SALEM: Yes, I'll be ready.

I saw I had a missed text from Amy apologizing that she wasn't holding last night but would have a new batch soon.

I got out of bed, pulled my panties out from between my cheeks, scratched the back of my head, and zombie-shuffled toward the bathroom. While on the toilet, I stretched my arms over my head, noticed the five o'clock shadow under my arms, and got a whiff of my skipped shower last night. Accompanying the melody of my pee stream was the scattering of all of the items on my sink as I leaned slightly to grab my toothbrush. My rinse cup fell to the floor. My Noxzema cleansing cream fell in the sink, and a bottle of Once-Daily Multi vitamins hit my foot.

With my toothbrush in my mouth, I pulled my panties up, flushed, fished the sink clean of all my hygiene products, and began getting ready to go out. "Oww," I grumbled as I brushed my hair and snagged it. I smiled in the mirror, "Fuck it," I skipped the flossing, didn't need it today… and if I had– I'd still have skipped.

I was going to a drug dealer's house, so who was I trying to impress?

I hand-fluffed my hair. "It's alive! It's alive!" I told my mirror self. Cell in hand, I typed:

A few seconds passed, then she replied:

I just shook my head at her whimsical way with

words, went to the living room, and sat on the couch, waiting.

"So, ya sure he'll have the same ones I took?"

Matty snorted. "Elementary, my dear Watson. What do ya think? He's a fuckin' drug dealer."

"Yeah, I know."

"It's alright to be nervous; it is a little heavier than pot. Just be cool." Cool, I thought, be cool like Elmore Leonard.

I was trying to be cool, but as we made our way across the street, I managed to trip on the curb of the sidewalk. As I fell, Matty caught hold of me and saved me from toppling over. We seemed to dance a few steps as we stumbled together until our feet became one with the ground.

"Whoo, careful, Dewey," Matty readjusted her glasses.

"Shut up, Gale. We're both just as clumsy; haven't you seen the movies?" I said through an embarrassed smile.

We both rolled our eyes at each other and began to walk again. I was hoping it wasn't much further to the dealer's house.

"Not much longer, trust me. I wouldn't walk if it was."

"Oh, I know you wouldn't."

"What's that supposed to mean?" asked Matty.

"Come on," I looked at her in a you're-kidding way, "you're one of the laziest people I know."

"I'm not lazy," she smiled, "I just like to conserve energy."

"Yeah, alright."

"What?" She said with a flip of her hair. "I do."

Our laughter mixed with the noise of passing cars, revving engines, honking horns, and sounds of children playing tag football in a nearby park. As we neared an apartment building, it seemed to grow gradually quieter. We continued, keeping to the shade of a few big oaks that ran along the side of the apartment complex parking lot.

We sauntered down the road beside a patch of trees, caught up in our conversation about how Steve Hodges' singing was meant for church; that way they could all pray for it to stop. There was a small house with two-toned paint and what looked like a black garbage bag taped over a window. A car was backing out of the driveway that occupied a car on cinder-blocks as we turned to walk through the yard.

As we came closer to the shabby porch, I couldn't help but think I'd seen this house in *American History*

X. Besides the trash, it looked very similar. "What a dump."

"This," Matty said, "is the stuff dreams are made of."

"Oh, I'm sure, Sam Spade," I smirked.

"Well, nobody's perfect."

The front door began to crack open as we went up the steps, opening all the way the instant we were on the porch. I almost took a step back.

"Sup, Big John?" Matty asked.

Big John was a very fitting name because big was what he was. His shoulders were almost as wide as the door frame. His demeanor reminded me of John Malkovich's character in Con Air, which, needless to say, was a little intimidating.

"Matty," he motioned with his head, "come on in."

He eyed me from behind a pair of sunglasses, then pushed them up on his bald head, revealing a scar from the corner of his left eye to his temple. "Who are you?"

"Salem," I answered after swallowing. "I'm with her."

"She's cool," Matty threw in for good measure.

"Alright, alright, alright." He turned around as

he said that, and we followed him into his living room.

"What will it be?" he asked as he sat in front of a littered coffee table. Open on the table was a magazine with a very graphic picture of a girl engaged in sex with two men. The girl in the photos seemed very young-looking, but before any real thought could form, he flipped it closed and slid it underneath the table.

"A martini, shaken, not stirred," I blurted out, and Matty elbowed me.

Big John laughed, "I like you already, Salem." He pulled out a silver tray covered in little purple ovals, round peach-colored little scored tablets, and little pink-coated pills. Turquoise-blue tablets were in a clear bottle, along with white ones and yellow ones. "Vicodins, OxyContin, Valium, Percocet, Darvocets, even some Thorazine; hell, I even got some plain old tranquilizers if that's your cup of joe." He grabbed a bottle off the floor and shook it, "Almost forgot. Got some Xanax as well."

"Oxy and Percs are fine with me," Matty said.

Big John took a few of each she ordered and put them in a clear baggie. "Usual amount?" he inquired.

"Two more of each. Time to treat myself since I got extra."

"Here's a couple on the house," he said, running his eyes quickly up and down her.

"Thanks, I'll get ya back."

He only shook his head in response.

"You?" he nodded toward me.

"Just some Percocet for now."

"Newbie? I've never seen ya around." He didn't wait for an answer before picking up a small egg-shaped container. "Want to see the good way to do it unless she's shown ya."

"Go ahead, make my day." I tried making myself sound like I wasn't just going with it to impress, but being so new at this, I wanted to make an impression. He unscrewed the top off the container. The top had a smaller egg shape that went down into itself. "This is a crusher." He placed two of the reddish-colored pills into the bottom of the container and then placed the top back on. "This is less messy and the quickest way in my view of things." He unscrewed the top again, cleared a spot on the silver tray, and poured out what reminded me of the dust from Mars in Total Recall.

"You might like this," Matty said. "I'm not a big fan."

"She'll like it; I can see it in her eyes," he laughed.

"Just joking with ya, sport. So, want a line?"

I watched him spread the pile with a playing card and gather it into small lines.

"Sure."

I watched him lean over the pile, pinch one of his nostrils shut as he ran the other along the length of the line closest to him; it was also the thickest line. I could see the powder go up into his nose like a vacuum cleaner.

Rising up, wiping his nose, "It'll shoot ya to the moon, man."

"E.T. phone home," I mumbled as he slid the tray toward me. I tried my best to mimic Big John's actions, but as soon as my nostril inhaled some, I sat up quickly, holding my nose as a few grains of the crushed pill fell out.

"Whoa! My nose is on fire."

"That's normal; it's a good burn, though, just like whiskey. C'mon, finish the line."

I stared at the rest of my remaining line and rubbed my nose with a knuckle. I sniffed one more time before leaning over again. I inhaled the rest in one quick movement with my head, trying to go with the Band-Aid theory and do it fast. I could already feel the drainage in the back of my throat as if I had a head cold, the taste was bitter, the texture chalky, but it was all good because I knew the high would be great.

Sitting up, I held my finger up to my nose as if I were holding back a sneeze or smelling something rank.

I sniffed one more time, then coughed into my hand.

"I'm good," I said after another cough and sniffle. I pointed at the other line, "I'll have two of those."

"That's the spirit," Big John laughed. "Matty?"

"I'll have what she's having." Matty slid the offered tray closer to herself.

"Now it's a good time," Big John said as Matty leaned in to do her line, and he placed his hand on her shoulder.

Yesterday was the highest I've ever been. It felt great, and the rush hit me fast and hard. It was all a new and exciting thing, as if it were a stoner's first adventure of getting high.

I enjoyed it.

No, I loved it.

Those two adjectives were probably why I was cutting a line of crushed Percocet on the corner of the

Casanova Theater's bathroom sink. After snorting the line, I checked myself in the mirror, making sure there was no dust left in my nostril and wiped my nose after sniffing hard one final time.

I had a little over an hour before I had to go into the projection booth and start pleasing the audience with our Western double feature, so before I met the Man of the West with Gary Cooper or got Cold Vengeance from John Wayne, I wanted to warm myself up some. I grabbed my purse, checked my nose again, and walked out of the restroom, and went outside.

Sunshine streamed down out of a nearly cloudless sky, filling the air with the washed-out light of late autumn. There was a little nip in the air, a hint of winter on the rise, but I could also smell the cut grass and dried leaves nearby.

I walked down Sunset Avenue, where it turned to Church Street, to the small restaurant Hop's BBQ, stepped inside, and bought a large coffee. Taking my coffee outside, I sat on a bench near the library-owned used bookstore. The day was pretty. The cool snap of a chill is just a whisper on the back of the breeze. I sipped my coffee thoughtfully, warmed my hands on the cup, and watched people walk here and there, in and out of stores, coming and going, all up and down the sidewalk.

Flea Musketeer was having a discount sale, along with Airbrush F/X. With Thanksgiving a week away, shop windows were covered in snowflakes, elves, more than one Santa, and snowmen, trying to put people in the holiday spirit and preparing for Christmas.

"Yo, Adrian," came from beside me as I was focused on watching a young woman across the street struggling to put a box in her car. I looked at Lily as she sat down beside me.

I pointed at myself, "You talking to me?"

"Yeah," she flipped her braids to the side. "Nobody puts Baby in a corner." She looked at me and patted the bench, "Well, nobody puts Baby on a street corner is probably more fitting, huh?" she grinned, and I couldn't help but grin with her.

"Yeah, I guess. Just trying to warm up a little." I lifted my coffee to add emphasis to my being cold.

She brushed at a couple of braids, ungluing them from her forehead and tucking them behind her ear. A new piece fell back in the same place she'd brushed; she tucked it ruefully.

"Ready for tonight?" I asked.

"Yeah, I guess. Steve's doing that '80s ticket cost tonight, though, so it'll probably be busy."

"At least it's not '60s night costing less than a dollar." I smiled. "Or a '20s ticket that would be worse. It'd be about twenty-seven cents, then he'd have to buy more chairs," I laughed.

"Yeah, I guess that'd be worse," she smiled at me. "You're full of random facts."

"Just movies, mainly."

"That's where you work, so I guess it's necessary, right?"

"Not really, but I like movie trivia." I took a sip of my coffee.

"Tell me something else."

"About what?"

"Anything, come on," she grinned eagerly.

"Uh, popcorn was first served in 1912 at movie theaters, but the first full-length film wasn't until a year later."

Lily laughed, "I love it, so random."

"Now you're making fun."

"No, seriously, not every day you learn something like that, ya know?"

"Been holiday shopping?" I pointed at the bag she was carrying.

"A little bit," she smirked. "Close your eyes."

"What?"

"Close your eyes," she said a little more sternly.

I closed them but felt stupid and told her so.

"Shut up. Open."

She was holding a book in front of my face.

"What is this?"

"It's a copy of Quentin Tarantino's Cinema Speculation. Hopefully, you like it; I know you dig movies and all things film, so here ya go."

"No, I haven't read it. It looks badass, though," I smiled.

"Well, enjoy."

"Thank you. This is awesome, seriously. Thank you."

"You're welcome."

After taking another mouthful of coffee, I asked, "You coming up to the booth tonight?"

"Maybe," She glanced up quickly. "I'll come up once I'm caught up."

"'Kay. I'll be up there."

"See ya later, Salem," she said as she got up and left me with my half-empty coffee cup.

Later in the projection booth, I grunted and cussed aloud with no worry of being heard behind the (having just learned) sound-proof walls of the booth and lifted the heavy-as-hell hexagonal steel cases of tonight's reels. When you learn that a projector runs through six feet of reel in a second, ten frames a foot, sixty frames a second; you realize why these damn things weigh so much.

I kinda wanted another pill. I wanted to get a little higher. I was starting to come down, so why not. It felt good. I felt good when I was high. The idea buzzed in my mind like a swarm of bees from Candyman, and I closed my eyes against the persistent whine of the thought. I had to keep my head tonight; I couldn't watch for the right-hand corner cigarette burns at the top of the screen if I was nodding off. The cigarette burns came twice. First, when there was only two minutes of film left, then when there was only five seconds. The five-second warning was when you got ready to shut one projector lens and open another.

"Come in!" I called out to the knock at the door.

"Brought ya a Coke," Lily placed the can on the

table next to me. "I talked John into doing the tickets tonight so I could chill up here. Told him I was trying to learn the projector better."

I was focusing on the latches on the case; one was refusing to cooperate. "Hope that was okay."

"Oh, yeah, sorry," I looked up. "Damn thing," I pointed at the case. "It's fine, kinda cool you want to be up here. It can get boring sometimes." The stubborn latch finally opened.

Looking up at her, our eyes locked. I couldn't help but think of that night, how she'd kissed me in this very room. I'd replayed her kiss over and over in my mind, causing me countless hours of confusion.

The memory froze, crystallized in my mind, and hung like a shard of ice, but her warm smile was melting the thought, threatening to make it fall out of my mouth, to cause me to voice my-

"Kiss me again," I blurted out.

I watched her expression change.

Fuck.

Fear gripped me. I'd ruined it, hadn't I? You're not supposed to tell a coworker to kiss you, even if she already had, and especially if it makes you a lesbian. Not even if she's become a friend, especially if she's a

friend. Fuck!

I gulped, "I'm sorry, I was just thinking out loud, I was-"

"What did you say?" she edged closer.

My stomach did a small flip-flop. Her voice was calm. Her eyes looked at me as though I had just given her a map to the Holy Grail.

"I said," I swallowed, "I said, you should kiss-"

This time, the flip-flop was more a series of cartwheels as her lips pressed against mine.

The kiss, which was tentative at first, bloomed like a flower. I felt her tongue touch my lower lip and met it, shyly at first, with my own. My hands covered her back, then slowly slipped around her front.

My hands were shaky and hesitant as I explored something new. I drew my hands back only to find them being guided back by hers, giving me permission to continue.

I touched her breasts, shy to begin with, then with some confidence, I slid my palms up their lower slopes to the tips. She uttered a small, moaning sigh directly into my mouth.

She slipped a hand up to my left breast, squeezed gently, and felt my heart speeding under it. Her other hand went to my hair and combed along the side of it. "Why are you crying?"

"I'm so confused," I admitted. "All my life, I was told that stuff like this was wrong, but how can it be when it's the only thing that feels right? I just, I don't know. I-"

She stopped my words with her kiss. At first just letting myself be kissed... and then I was kissing her back, kissing her without abandon. She wiped the wetness from beneath my eyes with soft little sweeps of her thumbs, then slipped her palms up my cheeks as I longed for her to do.

"It's okay. You got me now."

I slid my arms around her neck, my open mouth on hers, holding her and kissing her as deeply as I could.

The fragrance of her breath fueled my desire, the sweet line of her body pressed against mine.

My hands were still shaky as we began to part, my lips still warm and moist from her kiss. I knew the seats would start to fill up soon and didn't want to disappoint the audience, so regretfully, I took a step away from her before I had a chance to do what I wanted to do instead.

"I gotta get back to work," I said with a weak smile, still fighting tears of happiness.

"Yeah, you do. Stop being lazy, get to work; what ya think you're part of, Clerks?" she joked.

I gave a small laugh while going back to setting up the reel-to-reel. I began to think that maybe stuff like this wasn't just for the movies.

After the movie was over, I made my way down and found Lily. It felt like all of my courage was gone upon catching sight of her. I caught up to her as she was heading toward the exit.

"You think you could eat?" I blurted.

"Is this your way of asking me out on a date?" she smiled.

"Yeah, I guess it is," I said, now realizing how nervous I was.

"Well, then, if you put it that way. Of course, I would like to go on a date with you."

"Cool, I know a good place nearby. It's one of my favorite joints."

"Lead the way, Salem."

We were able to walk the five blocks to Geraldine's Soul Food. The bright purple neon sign was even more dazzling than when I usually come. I had never been here at night.

We entered hand in hand. Oh shit, I just realized

her hand was in mine. When did that happen? Oh god, it felt good, yet I was still fearful of what others thought all of a sudden. I withdrew my hand and played it off with an itch of some sort and didn't offer it back.

Now, I was fearful she was offended. Damn, I just couldn't win right now in my mental tennis match.

The restaurant was small and neat, with purple seating upholstery and walls covered in family pictures of the owner that traced back many generations, giving it a welcoming and familiar feel.

We chose a back table. When we sat down, I was struck by just how beautiful she was. The light was just right, and her skin was glowing like deep brown onyx in the sunset.

Oh shit, this felt nice, even though I had a feeling it shouldn't, or at least I've been told it shouldn't. I just needed to focus on right now, on her.

"So, you have me here. What do you want to talk about first?" she asked, exposing an adorable tiny gap in her smile that I just noticed.

A young girl dropped some change in the jukebox, and I was about to say something most likely embarrassing, but the song 'I Believe' came on over the speakers, saving me from the embarrassing mishap

I felt was to come.

"Brian McKnight," I blurted out.

"What do you know about Brian McKnight?" she teased.

"This is from Daddy's Little Girls," I said, as if everyone should know this.

"Wow, I'm impressed. You didn't strike me as a Tyler Perry fan."

"I just like good movies. He makes good movies. I know my films."

"Oh, you do, do you? Alright, 'Tell Me Why' by 8ball and MJG?"

"Hustle and Flow."

"'Big Pimpin'" by Tha Dogg Pound?"

"Above the Rim."

"Damn, alright, alright, one more, 'More Bounce to the Ounce' by Zapp and Roger."

"Blue Hill Avenue, any more brain busters?" I laughed.

"That could have been Any Given Sunday as well."

"Yeah, and that happens a lot, so I just gave the first movie that comes to mind."

"One more, one more," she was smiling so hard,

"I promise the last one."

"Alright, give it to me."

"I've Had The Time of My Life"

"Oh, of course, Dirty Dancing, but Jordan Peele made it so creepy in Get Out, and I also think of Family Guy in their Star Wars parody," I answered with a smile to rival hers.

"Okay, respect. I like your answers."

"Did I pass?"

"Of course you did. What do you want as a prize?"

I gave a brief pause and then gathered enough courage to say, "I already got mine." I reached over across the table and took her hand in mine. Butterflies fluttered in my stomach, and then the mood was interrupted as the waitress came to take our orders.

As we waited for our food, we talked. We got to learn more about each other. We discussed movies, music, books, and our likes and dislikes in society as a whole.

We enjoyed this moment together. Moments like these were hard to come by. Moments like these were when we were at our happiest. When you find that person, that makes all your other troubles slip into the background of your mind, and gives you the chance to take a breath. Pure, undiluted joy was a hidden chance to forget how tattered you felt like you were. This wasn't explainable; it was just an experience you had to find on your own.

After we ate, we walked back toward the theater.

"Where are you parked? I'll walk you," I said.

"I was hoping you would."

We walked and talked a little more as we made our way to her car. Once there, we stood beside the driver's door. She seemed to be at ease, and I was a little more awkward, not knowing what to do.

After a few seconds, she said, "A romantic dinner and a walk to my car in the moonlight; there is only one thing that would make it better."

"What is tha-"

Her mouth interrupted my question with the answer. Her lips parted. I fell inside her warmth. Her tongue was stiff at first, teasing me, playing with my awkwardness, it seemed. Our eyes were open. I felt her breath as she softly laughed, and I saw in her eyes all good teasing, no meanness at all – and I felt at ease. Our eyes closed together, and our tongues began to do a slow and groovy slow dance.

I relished the taste. I savored the feeling. I was amazed by our rhythm as if we had been doing this forever.

I leaned away, but she pulled me back and kissed me deeper before breaking away.

"Have a good night, Salem," she said as she got into her car.

"I will, you too."

Wow, she definitely was in my head now. Her perfume seared in my nostrils. I felt completely cut open, vulnerable, yet happy. I felt fragile and yet... tranquil.

This is who I am.

I am a girl who likes girls.

It felt great to admit it to myself. I was still a little fearful, though, of the idea of being open, but only time could tell on that one. For now, I needed to get home and get some rest.

TATTERED

8

Breathe easy.

I try to see myself as you would right now. Wearing jeans and a loose-fitting shirt, an unspoken concession to my habit, and my hair looking as if no brush had passed through it at any time in recent memory. Why should you believe me?

I'm telling you the truth.

Yes, I know what it sounds like.

I let my thoughts drift. My memory of times and places when I felt at peace and there hadn't been any worry those were distant and faded. My childhood was a blur, bouncing back and forth between schools. My youth is a jumbled collection of disconnected faces and events, having to raise myself after my parents' death. Even the years as a young adult, from before Lily, were no longer clear in my mind. My entire life was lost to me. I had given it all away. Lily was helping me, allowing me to learn that when we are able to see our past a sad story then we find out who we are today. The past only gets *you to right now, but it doesn't* make *you who you are right now.*

Yes, I love her.

I swallow hard before restarting the telling of the story that brought me here. **Breathe easy.**

When I awoke the following morning, the sun was streaming so brightly through my window that I thought I might have overslept. Lily and I had spent hours after the movie talking at the restaurant. I glanced over at the window and realized that the reason it was so bright was that I had forgotten to draw the blinds. I laid my head back on my pillow, still disoriented, my body refusing to get out of bed. There were muffled sounds of traffic on the street.

I rolled over on my side, looked at the alarm clock, and scratched my thigh. I finally got up, crossing my fingers that there was some instant coffee and/or some pot.

I checked my little tin box with the same

Mooby's sticker I'd put on my freshman year of high school. No weed was inside. I groaned in protest and made my way to the kitchen, rubbing sleep out of my eyes, only to find an instant coffee can full of nothing but residue of the contents no longer there. I groaned again in complaint at my crummy day thus far.

Well, at least I can still take a shower.

My shower was an amazing refresher; it helped me wake up and overlook the shitty start to my day. I picked up my toothbrush and toothpaste, squeezed the tube, and got a great glob of nothing out of it.

"Oh, come on!" I grumbled. "What else is going to go wrong?" I used some mouthwash, hoping it would do. Then, I brushed my hair. I went to the living room, thinking that maybe some television would help me think about anything but my shitty day so far.

The first thing I heard from the TV was that famous, often-used pickup line from "Jerry Maguire": "You had me at 'hello.'"

I switched channels, and "Hello, gorgeous" blared out from "Funny Girl." The line got me thinking of Lily. I liked her.

I really liked her.

I pushed the up button on the remote, and "Marathon Man" asked me, "Is it safe?"

I wasn't sure if it was, I thought, but I'm willing to try if she is. Aren't I? I hope she likes me the same way. She must, right? She has to because, hell, she kissed me.

Changing the channel again, "Moonstruck" yelled for me to "Snap out of it!" as I absentmindedly surfed more stations.

I shook the spiderwebs from my head that had caught my mind wandering and turned the television off. I threw the remote on the coffee table, and at the same instant of plastic smacking wood, my phone cried out with "Helen's Theme," announcing an incoming call.

"Hello?"

"Mornin' bitch," Matty greeted.

"Hey, what's up?"

"Nothing much. I got some extra dough and was wondering if ya wanted to party a little."

"I guess I could use a little pick-me-up."

"I believe we all can." Matty said, "I'll be there in a little. We'll swing by Big John's place, that cool with ya?"

"Yeah, sure."

"Better be; I'd hate to have to take ya by force," she laughed. "Well then, may the force be with you," I joked.

"Oh yeah. Anyway, see ya in a little bit."

"Alright."

I ended the call and squeezed my phone back into my jeans pocket. I was glad I didn't have to text Amy to score some pot and could save myself from her terrible one-liners, even though she was actually pretty cool herself. After smelling my underarms and putting on some deodorant, Wednesday's cello rang out of my pocket.

It was a text from Lily:

LILY: Hey :) wht u doin? I was thinking about u and last nite ;) Could we get 2gether l8er?

I texted back:

SALEM: Maybe tonight after work -_- I'm busy right now.

Her reply came quickly, and a swarm of butterflies let loose in my belly:

LILY: CAN'T WAIT! :-@ <3

I slid my phone into my pocket and tried my best to think about all that happened last night. A little was blurry, but all was great. I knew I kissed her, that's for sure, and she kissed me, and I liked it—better yet, I loved it. I was hoping she'd kiss me again tonight or somehow right this moment.

I began to worry then. How would people see me? What would they think if I was in a relationship with another girl? How would Matty react? Or worse, would my boss, Steve, be okay with two of his employees in a relationship—two female employees?

I tried my best to swallow my fear and trust in what Lily had said: "It'll be okay." I believed her. The way I felt just thinking about last night was nothing but the truth to those very words.

I'd been waiting for Matty nearly twenty minutes when I began to get clammy and sweaty. Was it nerves? Something else? My head started to hurt, starting out as a dull throb and escalating steadily to a gut-churning pounding. I was shocked at how badly I felt all at once. Then it began to fade for a little while, then slowly came back, like bad cramps, coming and going, good to bad to worse. I felt like shit. I just wanted to get high. How long has it been? What was it I was truly taking anyway? Could you get sick this quickly? I wanted to get high enough that this would all go away. Getting high will help this; I knew it would.

I took the time I had waiting to pull up some information on my phone. I read that opioid withdrawal can occur as soon as eight hours after your last use, and meth can start after one day. Alcohol was six hours; pot could be a day after; hell, even caffeine had a withdrawal time starting at twelve hours after your last cup.

During a brief spell of feeling mildly human at best while willing myself to feel good, I answered Matty's knock.

"Brr," Matty chattered out and shivered. "That sun is a liar! I'd only be colder if I'd fucked an icicle." Closing the door, she said, "Whoa, you look rougher than Charlie Sheen after a coke binge."

"Thanks," my voice dripped with sarcasm.

Matty took a step back and waved her hand in front of her nose. "Damn, I'm trying to process what you said, but I lost my thought after getting hit with that breath. That shit's kicking like a Swayze Roadhouse."

I gasped, "What, really?"

"Nah, just joking, but you were about to do a breath check, huh?"

"You bitch," I laughed.

"Only on days that end in y." She sat her purse on the coffee table and pulled out an orange prescription bottle, popped the top off, and rolled the last two pills on the table like a pair of dice. "Before we go, I thought we could get the party started early."

"I'm not complaining," I said, wanting this terrible feeling to go away before she saw through my pitiful attempt of playing it off. I didn't want to seem like I couldn't handle it after saying I was going to go.

She lit a cigarette and took a deep drag.

"I heard that shit will kill ya," I said.

"Well," she exhaled a puff of smoke, "if Billy Porter doesn't have to give up butts, neither do I." She put a piece of paper over the pills and used her lighter to crush them.

As I watched her crush the pills, I began to wonder if she was going through the same thing, and that was why she wanted to do a little before leaving to go to Big John's place. Did she look like she lost weight? And I didn't think it was as cold outside as she made it out to be. Was that a tremble in her fingers?

She cut me a line and handed me a straw made from a rolled-up dollar, and my brain thought of nothing else but those thin white lines. My nose ran over the intricate cut of powder. It was bliss, I thought, a perfect representation. How could there be any better feeling than knowing all of your worries can disappear so easily?

"Hey," Matty said, "hear 'bout Chan?" She left the question hanging, not wanting to reveal the whole story of what she knew or how she acquired such gossip. "Well," she began, "I heard Steve caught him smoking a blunt of loud behind the theater the other week, and that's why he hasn't been showing up."

"Really?"

"Yeah, yeah, but the good part," she laughed, "the good part is he tried to offer him a hit. Then started crying and begging to not get fired when Steve took it and threw it down."

"Well, he was asking for it, I guess. Why smoke at work? Do that stuff at home, dude."

"True that," she laughed, then yawned. "I'm tired. I was up all night watching Lisbeth so my parents could go out."

"How old again?"

"Well, to her, it's seven and a half, almost eight."

I smiled, "She's cute."

"Yeah, but she's maybe a lesbo. Think she's

crushing on ya," she laughed. "She keeps asking if you'll visit again."

"Guess she liked the braids I did on her," I smirked.

"Better than mine. I gotta learn, but I can't follow that shit," she pointed at her hair, "as it shows."

"It's not that bad."

"It's a rat's nest."

"A well-kept rat's nest," I clarified.

"Come on, let's bounce."

IMAX (an acronym for Image Maximum) has the capacity to record and display images of far greater size and resolution than conventional film systems, and that's how I felt while walking with Matty – as if I had IMAX format vision. I could see, feel, taste, smell, and god knows what else… everything.

I know that this was a misconception, but at the moment, I didn't care if it was true or not. I was only enjoying the feeling.

"That's fucking gross," Matty muttered in discontent.

"What?" Apparently, being able to see it all wasn't true.

She pointed across the street at a couple holding hands and laughing.

"What makes you sickened by happiness?" I jokingly asked.

"Nah, just disgusted by faggots."

That was when I noticed the cheerful couple, who were now kissing, were both men. They looked happily unconcerned, as if just being with each other made a sometimes ugly world beautiful again.

"Really?" I asked, looking back toward her after watching the couple break their embrace and resume walking.

"Damn right," she made a gagging sound. "Anyway, here we are."

The garbage bag that had covered the window was gone, replaced by a new window. The paint was now all one shade, and the porch steps didn't wobble or threaten to cave in as we used them.

Big John answered the door in no time after Matty knocked. "Matty, Salem. Come on in," he waved us in, and we followed him to his living room.

As we sat down, Matty said, "Oh, Big John, I may have to discuss a little bit of a problem with ya."

"Yeah, sure. But first, check this shit out." He

pulled out a vacuum-sealed bag, broke it open, and slid out a regular plastic baggie. Untying the knot, he poured out some bud that looked like gold from the yellow shade sparkling from its crystals. "Sticky and stinky is the way I like 'em. This weed is the best you'll ever smoke." He produced a heavy-walled clear pipe from under the table. "I gotta share, this shit's so good."

"That shit stinks," Matty said.

"That's a good thing," I said.

"Damn right, it is," Big John agreed.

He packed the bowl and handed it to me, offering me the first toke, what's known as the 'green hit.'

"Really?"

"Sure, no worries, it's free of charge," he said with a wink.

The glass was cold on my lips but quickly began to warm as I put the lighter's flame to the weed. Now for a steady inhale, tasting the sweetness and smoothness of the smoke as it entered my lungs, I could hear the crackle of the bud burning. As I held the smoke inside, I could feel the effects already taking hold, starting from the top of my head and as I exhaled, ending at the tips of my toes. My whole body was relaxed and weightless.

"Whoa," I managed to say, handing the pipe back.

"I know. That shit was dipped in honey oil, pretty much straight THC."

"Whoa," was all I could muster once again.

Big John turned toward Matty and placed a hand on her knee; through the fog of my high, I heard him say, "Come on, we'll go discuss that problem."

I watched Matty get up almost reluctantly and follow him out of the room. I sat back on the couch, feeling myself succumb to the tingle; my entire body went numb.

"Whoa," I said one more time.

Cut scene, that's a wrap.

"Come on, let's go," Matty said.

I had already been fighting sleep and my eyelids felt anchored down with the weight of sleep, but they fluttered open to her voice.

"What?" I asked. "Ya got both, or I gotta wait?"

"I got it," her voice cracked mid-sentence. "Come on."

"Alright," I said, pushing myself off the couch.

We headed out and started our way toward the

theater. I checked my cell and realized we had been there a couple of hours. It was almost time for us to go to work.

"Wow," I slid my phone back in my pocket, "what took us so long?"

"Well, while you were nodding off, I handled a debt with John. He gave you yours as a freebie."

"Freebie?"

"Yeah, but trust me, don't ever ask for a loan."

"Why? He doesn't seem too bad."

"Just don't, alright," Matty said. "So, what's playing tonight?"

I scratched my head, "Umm… oh, The Big Boss with Bruce Lee. Ya know that one, right?"

"Nope, I'm not much for hand-chopping, leg-punch, stunt-wire movies."

"Well, it was his first smash hit. It's about a guy who starts working at a nice factory and then finds out they sell heroin."

"Sounds boring. This weekend is good, though."

"Yeah, The Terminator. It's a Schwarzenegger classic."

"I really liked Commando."

Matty began to stumble but caught her balance. I heard her hiss between her teeth.

"You alright?" I asked.

"Yeah, yeah, I'm cool. Just sore," she paused just long enough for me to notice, "…guess from all this damn walking." She didn't sound convincing, but I let it go.

"I enjoy walking."

"It's nice, but I can't wait 'til the 'mom' lets me borrow the keys to the car again."

I grinned, "I keep forgetting you're only seventeen."

"Well, I don't act it, and they don't treat me like it either. Hell, every time they do it always leads back into the old argument of 'I'm only a check to you, I'm not your kid.' So, they give me my space. But, next month, I'm eighteen, and I'll be outta there."

Before I knew it, we were at work going our separate ways. She went behind the concession stand and began her corn kernel-popping ritual. I went up the stairs and into the projection booth.

I was welcomed inside by the sound of Steve rummaging through the reel-to-reel cases on the shelves.

"Damn, I can't find it."

"What?"

"The Lee flick. I was sure we had it." He looked through another row of bulky steel cases, "Well, luckily, we only advertised Lee's name. Guess we'll show Game of Death or Fists of Fury. Your pick."

"The first one. It was his last, ya know."

"I think I heard that once." He handed me the first case, "Here ya go."

I took the case to the table and then began setting up the camera. After lugging the rest of the cases over, Steve set up the other camera.

"When's our next double feature?"

"It's up to you," he looked up with a smile. "You've worked hard, so I'll let you pick the day and the films. Just…I would like the movies to be somewhat relatable."

"Sure, but really?" I was surprised by the opportunity he was giving me. "Thank you. This is awesome. I'll pick some good ones, promise." Steve chuckled. "I knew you'd like the idea." He patted the projector as if it were a pet after he finished loading the film. "Guess I'll leave ya to it." "Yeah. Hey, thanks again."

"No problem, Salem, you earned it," he said, opening the door to leave. After setting everything up properly with minimal hassle, I sat down, but as soon as my ass touched the seat of the chair, a knock came from the door. "Open the pod bay doors, please HAL." Her voice was muffled through the crack of the door as she opened it slowly, trying to be sneaky. I knew it was Lily before she even walked in with a smile on her face. Her braids were undone, and her hair was big and natural.

"Ya know, I was just thinking," I said. "Why don't you come up sometime and see me?"

"Really," she smiled, "and I was just wondering how full of shit you are."

I raised my head with a laugh, "Oh, really now."

"Gotta Coke for ya," she placed the can on the table, "if you get thirsty."

"Thanks." She had told me before that she liked my useless movie knowledge, so I let one rip, "Ya know," I nodded toward the drink, "cup holders weren't in theaters until 1981 when AMC Theaters introduced them." "Guess they weren't expecting drinks and snacks to be a huge part of the movie-going experience."

"Well, nearly thirty percent of the money brought in by theaters comes from their junk food."

"Really," showing genuine amusement, "I guess I gotta get into the concession business."

"Yeah, the profits are great when the expense is only about four percent of that."

"Well, that settles it. I'm going to the snack bar."

I turned my head toward her, "No, ya can't." I then began fiddling with a few of the knobs and buttons, getting everything properly set up so I could go about showing the movie without worry of malfunctions. I sat down next to her, pointing at the camera, "You can't even work that."

"True, true."

My hands rested on my knees, but my fingertips seemed to have a mind of their own as they timidly inched closer to her knee until I was touching her bare skin.

She placed her hand on mine. "Salem, you don't have to be... to be afraid."

"But," I looked down, unsure, then looked back up. "I am. This... this is... it's so-"

"I know."

"Why are you so confident?" innocence is

apparent in my question.

Her lips curved upward in a sweet smile. "Salem, you aren't the first girl I've been with." She squeezed my hand with reassurance. "I know who I am and what I want."

I turned to face her, and she instinctively wrapped her arms around me, holding me. As my arms slid up her back, my cheek rested on her shoulder.

"Hey," she kept her hands on my shoulders as she pulled away, "I got something I wanna show ya."

"What is it?"

"After work, I mean."

"Okay." I pulled her back into the embrace that I not only wanted but needed.

Too soon... we let go.

It was time for the movie.

"You gotta be kidding me," my voice shook with fear.

"What?" she playfully shoved me. "Come on, trust me."

I really wanted to trust her, but I couldn't extinguish my expanding horror as I looked up at the rusted (and probably old, loose, brittle, and ready-to-fall) ladder that led to the roof of the Casanova Theater.

"I don't like heights."

"It's sturdy; look, I'll show you," she began to climb. She went up a little before saying, "Come on, Salem, trust me."

"Trust me, trust me," I muttered over and over as I grabbed a rung with a trembling hand. I looked up at how swiftly she was making her way up the ladder and finally started climbing up with her... ...then we were on the roof.

The night was clear, cloudless, and gorgeous. Stars glittered across the arc of the sky in an extravagant, misty sprawl of light.

I looked across town to the west and saw the pulsing lights of Club Enigma. Beyond those were the twinkling gridwork of orange that marked the courthouse and the small, new housing development on the far side of the library.

"Beautiful, isn't it?" she asked before running near the ledge, spreading her arms wide, and yelling, "I'm the King of the world!" She spun around, looking at the awestruck expression I wore at all the lights. She ran back to me, laughing, and pulled me close to her. "But," she bit her lip, "it isn't as beautiful as you."

"Lily," I closed my eyes for a second, "this is all so new, and I don't know if I can."

"Just answer me this, okay?"

"Yeah, sure."

She gently moved her hands down my arms, lacing our fingers together. "What's wrong with this?"

My lip quivered while I searched for an answer that wasn't there. "You don't... you just don't understand," I said angrily, fighting my own emotions surging through my heart while all of society's bigotry against them ran through my head.

"You think I don't understand? You really think that?" she asked, letting me go. "I understand Salem, I do. When I came out, did you think my dad wanted a lesbian daughter? No, he didn't, so he disowned me. My mother wasn't around much anyway, but it pushed her completely away. My so-called best friend no longer even wanted to remember how to be a friend. All of this because of something I couldn't control, something I didn't choose to be. You think honestly I woke up one morning and just wanted everyone I knew to pretend they didn't know me?"

Now she was crying, and her expression of utter, abject sorrow nearly broke my heart. I took her back into my arms. I stroked the back of her head, my fingers running through the thick curls of her hair. The thumb of my other hand brushed her cheek, trailing behind her ear. I stared into her eyes, watery with the memory of the same pain and confusion I felt. I pulled her closer, my fingers tracing the line of her jaw, caressing her bottom lip, then I leaned in close enough to feel her breath. "I'm sorry. I didn't know. I guess you do understand."

She closed her eyes and I took the moment to gather my courage and pressed my lips to her. After a moment, our lips parted, and our eyes slowly opened as if waking up from a pleasant dream.

"This feels right. It has to be," I whispered.

"It is."

Who leaned in first? I don't know, but our mouths found each other once more. I parted her lips with my tongue; she twirled hers around mine. Our hands begin to explore. Lily's hands ran up my side as mine pulled her closer, pulling her face closer to mine. When her fingertips traced my nipples through my bra, the heat between my legs flared suddenly and urgently.

"Lily," I whispered desperately through panting breaths, "I never-"

"Been with a black girl?" her lips formed a grin.

"No, with anyone," I confessed with a smile. "Your skin doesn't matter, silly."

"I know that I was only teasing ya," she looked

at me with such passion and concern. "We don't have to," she said, "I'll understand." "I know, but…I want to."

"Are you sure?"

"Yes," I pulled her closer. "I'm ready"

We'd gone to my apartment. It was closer and though I was equal parts excited and nervous, I couldn't wait to be alone with Lily and continue what we'd started on the roof. Right now, she lay deeply asleep with what looked like a faint smile on her lips. Her pillowy curls fluffed out on the bed as well as partly on my shoulder. I could still feel her fingers on my bare stomach, trailing steadily downward. The feel of her fingers working their way underneath the waistband of my jeans seemed to have left a burn from the heat I had felt. The sight of her looking at me had been unbelievable.

My mind was a jumble of thoughts as I lay there.

I looked around my room. On a chair in the corner, haphazardly thrown, I could see Lily's bra and my panties. Smiling, I remembered how the rest of our clothes were scattered around my apartment.

I can still see her bra slowly slide off her breasts, the straps falling down her arms. I remember feeling the cool mattress under me, Lily looking at me as her fingers slid up my legs, and how she had pulled my panties away until I was completely naked.

I close my eyes, recalling the sensations of her tongue on my body, her kissing my breasts, down my stomach, and then slowly pushing my legs apart. A small tremor goes through me, remembering her tongue finding its way between my legs. A gentle kiss on my clit and I'd shivered, her tongue exploring, tasting, and I'd begun to break. When her fingers, one…then two… entered me and with her tongue still tasting– I'd flown.

I had arched my back, my hands gripping her hair, and rode one of the most incredible sensations I'd ever experienced.

I replayed every kiss imprinted on my skin, along my inner thigh, up my belly, between my breasts, all the way to my mouth.

I'd just had sex…with a *girl*.

Lily and I had sex, and it was…*amazing*.

I wanted that feeling again.

I wanted Lily.

"I love you," I whispered.

She pulled herself closer to me and placed her head in the crook of my neck. Her arms held me tightly as if she were afraid. I soon realized it was me that was scared. It was the first time I had ever said that to her. It was the first time I've ever said those words to anyone.

I kissed her as she stirred.

"Izzis a dream?" she asked, with sleepy sweetness.

"I think it might be."

"Good. Don' wake me up. I don' wannit ta end."

"Me either," I whispered to no-one as her breathing became more measured as she fell asleep.

Finally, my own mind faded to black.

9

Breathe easy.

Nervous sweat burned a dozen scrapes and stung my eyes. I felt the walls of hope crumbling around me. My hands trembled in front of me. Never before had I experienced such pain, for never before had I had any to share to this extent until now.

I take a deep breath to blow away the remnants of my self-pity. I have to tell it all. If not now, then when?

Where was I?

Oh, yeah. I remember now I was-

Yes, that's true, but it was a little more complicated than that. It was about two weeks or so after she stayed at my place for the night. It was after Thanksgiving, I know for sure.

I squeezed my eyes tightly shut, but tears escaped, nevertheless, trickling down my cheeks. I watch a couple fall on the tabletop.

I slowly open my eyes.

Breathe easy.

Sunshine teased between a crack in the overcast now and then. The sunlight wasn't much, and by noon, the day had actually grown darker. Distant thunder foretold a dreary afternoon.

"I'm as mad as hell, and I'm not going to take this anymore!" The television blared as I sat down, stirring a cup of instant coffee and humming the theme of Indiana Jones. I wasn't in the mood to watch "Love Jones," so I changed the channel. I saw Wesley Snipes in the final minutes of "Disappearing Acts"; since it was so close to the end, I turned the channel again. Eastwood's face appeared as the opening scene of "Coogan's Bluff" played. I decided to leave the remote alone this time. Clint has always been a favorite of mine. He has such an amazing film persona and is one hell of a director, not to mention he's such a badass he can blow bubbles with beef jerky.

I took a sip of my coffee and grimaced. It was

strong enough to eat away the porcelain cup but not strong enough to be able to stand without it. I was wiping my nose to clear away any pill dust that may have been there and was mid-sniff when my phone rang out with an incoming text. It was Matty.

I looked at the baggie on my coffee table; three were left inside. I typed:

I sent the text and decided to call Lily while I still held my phone. She picked up on the third ring.

"Hey you," Lily answered with bubbling excitement.

"Hey yourself," I said. "You sound wide awake; I'm still drinking coffee."

"I got up early. I had to help my grandma with a few errands. What you up to?"

"Nothing much, waiting on Matty and thinking

of you."

"Really? Of me, that's sweet," she laughed and blew me a phone kiss. "What are you and Matty gonna do?"

"Nothing really, just chill. She said she's never seen Eight-Legged Freaks, so might watch that. What are you doing now?"

"Watching my grandma rummage through packets of seed."

"Seeds?"

"Yeah, she's part of the garden club and takes pride in her flowers."

"That's cool, I guess. Are you ready for tonight?"

"What's tonight? I forgot," she joked.

"You forgot!" My anger is clearly fake. "It's my night to pick the features."

"Oh, yeah! Salem, I'm proud you got the chance," she said sincerely.

"Me too. You ready for it?"

"Of course, what are the flicks again?"

"Monkey Business and Gentlemen Prefer Blondes. They both star Marilyn Monroe."

"I like Marilyn. She's hot-"

"You are so gay-"

"Hey, do I need to remind you that you are-"

"No," I blew her a phone kiss, "remind me not, missy."

"Hope you and Matty have fun."

"It'd be better if you were here."

"Aren't you just a sweetie?"

I heard the knock on the door.

"Hey, well, Matty's here, so I'll see ya tonight," I said.

"Alright, babe, bye."

I put my phone on the coffee table as I called out, "Come on in!"

Matty came shuffling into the living room, barely able to pick her feet up. Sweat had built up on her forehead, a few strands of hair were stuck to her skin like paint.

"Oh, my god! You look-"

"Please, not now," the words came out as a labored whisper. "Where's it at?" she asked, practically falling onto the couch.

I nodded toward the baggie. Her trembling hand reached for it as I started to break apart some bud to pack a bowl.

"Don't worry, Salem. I'll be good here in a few."

She pulled out two of the pills and started crushing them. "You care if I do this here?"

"Go ahead," I said, not knowing why she asked.

I watched her pull out a small bundle of things I've never seen before.

"Can I use this?" pointing at last night's glass of water.

"Sure," I said, still watching curiously.

She shot water through a needle to make sure it worked or to clean it, I guessed, then she tapped the powder she collected on a folded playing card into a spoon. She added several drops of water from an eyedropper and yanked three matches out of a book of them and struck them. She moved the spoon over the match's flame. The odor of sulfur caused me to sneeze. She then sucked the liquid into the syringe through a cotton ball. A stream of blood shot up into the needle; she'd entered the vein. She pushed the contents into her veins, then pulled out. The syringe fell on the floor as she fell back into the couch.

Ten seconds, if that long, she sighed blissfully.

I heard the blood pounding inside my head. I felt the familiar pumping of adrenaline, my body's automatic response to the possibility of getting high. Everything seemed to start up all at once, all the customary expectations. I was surprised at how strong the need was, given the fact I just snorted half a pill not too long ago.

I watched her, feeling what the people of Walla Walla, Washington, must have felt like in 1928 while walking in The Liberty Theater for the first, 'talkies.' Her eyes fluttered, her lips parted; first came another sigh of bliss, then she asked me, "You wanna try?"

Watching her reaction, the pot I got from Amy last night didn't even seem interested anymore, no matter how good she said it was. With another look at Matty, I reached for the needle on the floor.

As the needle released into my arm, my mind became as locked down as the Vannacutt Psychiatric Institute for the Criminally Insane. It took a few moments to come to the realization that something was wrong. Or, maybe it was right. My mind went completely blank; then my vision went black. The world becomes a darkened haze.

My chest began to thump in agony, and I realized I had stopped breathing because of the pain. I began to shiver, and the chill grew with each breath. I felt warm, and the warmth turned into heat, which spread outward, covering my whole chest until the flaming heat succumbed to my body.

What happened next occupied mere minutes, but either my mind turned lightning fast, or the minutes played taunt, for it seemed it had been hours. I was hot.

I was cold.

I was as high as I've ever been.

Then, I became even higher than that.

Then, nothing. I blacked out completely.

"You're gonna need a bigger boat," Lily said. "I mean a bigger bag," she laughed. "Yeah, maybe," I said while placing the books I had found on a table already covered in them. We had been in The Bookworm for about ten minutes or so, and I had already found six books. "What's this? It kinda sticks out."

"Oh, this," I picked up the book, flipped the pages, and turned it over in my

hands, "this is No Beast So Fierce; it's an Edward Bunker book. I've been wanting

to try his stuff since I found out Quentin Tarantino was a fan. He played in

Reservoir Dogs as Mr. Blue is an amazing movie."

"Cool," Lily nodded her head, "I might check it out if it's good."

"This one was a movie with Dustin Hoffman."

"Good?"

"No idea, I haven't seen it." I picked that one up and another one written by

some guy with a hard-as-hell last name to pronounce; I remember the movie Fight

Club, so I might as well check the book out. I put the rest back on the shelf with

Lily's help. "So," her tone was serious, "when are you gonna tell people about us so we can stop hiding?"

"Lily," I let out a deep breath, "I want to. It's just so hard." I looked down,

ashamed at being scared, then looked up into her eyes, "I promise, soon."

"Okay," she caressed my arm as her hand went down to hold mine. "I'm sorry for pressing the issue-"

"No," I shook my head, "You're not. I completely understand you." She smiled, nodded, and quickly kissed me. Suddenly, as our lips pulled apart, a woman in a black coat and blue jeans came down the same aisle as us. Her hair, despite the gray, looked gorgeous, and her glasses were a stylish blue. She was holding what looked like ten cheap romance novels in her arms as she neared us. "Excuse us," Lily said.

"Excuse me," she said with a smile I recognized. She was the same woman who I'd met at the LGBTQ meeting, the one that gave me the flier. The one who told me to embrace my feelings. She caught my eye and gave me an unmistakable grin and a knowing nod but kept going her own way without a word. No words were needed; she knew I had taken her advice. "So, you never told me why you read so much," Lily broke the brief silence. "Oh," I collected myself. "It's just a great escape, the same as movies."

"Escape from what?"

I knew the question was innocent conversation, but it still cut deep as a surgeon's blade. I didn't like discussing my past, but didn't I owe her that?

Shouldn't I tell her? Shouldn't I trust her? I did trust her. "Okay, well," I began, "growing up wasn't always the best for me. My dad would drink when I was younger, and my mom was always in and out of my life. So, I had to care for myself in a lot of ways. I was a loner at school, kinda like a weird Gothic type. I was shy and into dark things like horror movies, Tim Burton, and true crime novels. I would wear dark clothes, and dark eyes, I looked like a cast member from Dark Shadows sometimes, and well, I just stood out as the weird kid. My dad was cool sometimes, but I didn't have a mom to talk to, and I didn't want to burden my dad with my teenage girl problems. I remember how-"

"Salem," her hand now holding my chin, our eyes locked, "You don't have to tell me." She kissed me. "I don't," I agreed. "But I want to," I kissed her back. "Anyway, my dad and mom would fight a lot when she was around, and he was sober, so I had to find something to do in my room. There's a little for now. I want you to know these things; I do. So, I will start opening up a little more."

"Me too, now come on, let's buy these books, huh?"

I wrapped my arms around her waist, pulling her back to my stomach, and kissed her neck to show my appreciation for her just being her. We headed to the front of the store to pay for the books to add to my ever-growing collection.

I had picked a Betty Boop skit to show before starting the Monroe films and was sliding the cartoon's case back on the shelf when I caught my foot on the edge of the steel rack. "Oww," I grumbled as I shoved the case into place. I got the opening credits rolling on the first movie before sitting down to inspect the damage to my foot. I untied my sneaker, rolled my sock off, and turned it over in my hands while massaging my toes. "Oww," I mumbled, looking at the scrape and what would be a decent-sized bruise.

"I'll kiss it and make it better," Lily said. She had snuck up on me while I was focused on my foot. She laughed at making me jump.

I looked up and smiled. "Mrs. Robinson, you're trying to seduce me. Aren't you?" I joked.

"Just a little bit," she winked. "I had to help John with the letter changer pole thingy on the marquee out front. You know, I don't think there's a name for that thing. Anyway, I'm free now and thought you'd need my help. I also brought a Coke and Sloth's favorite candy bar, the Baby Ruth... thought you could use some chocolate."

"Well, thank you," I said, putting my sock and shoe back on. "Have you ever seen this?"

"Nope."

"It's an okay musical comedy. This was the main one that made her seem like a 'dumb blonde' type. It was based on a book by Anita Loos. The best song is 'Diamonds Are a Girl's Best Friend.'"

"Interesting."

"I can be smart when it's important, but most men don't like it. That was something she said once."

"Well, I like it," she said, walking close to me. "I've been thinking." She was standing in front of me, our knees touching. "Well, not really thinking. It's more so fantasizing," she stepped closer, enclosing my legs inside hers. She sat on my lap.

"Fantasize, huh?" I teased, my breath already heavy.

"Oh, yeah," her arms wrapped around my neck, her hands interlocked in my hair. Watching me with eyes that glittered, rolling her shoulders provocatively.

After a minute, Lily stood, moved between my legs, and gently pushed them open. Slowly she went to her knees, placing one hand on my waist, the other on my face, pulling me to the edge of my chair and in for a kiss. She nibbled and teased me while my breath became shallower. Her fingers worked their way under my shirt, pushing it up until I felt cool air on me. Lily moved back and slowly pulled my bra cup aside, and placed her lips on my nipple. I was arching involuntarily, my legs wrapped around her as she gently sucked. I couldn't get close enough to her and felt the delicious powerlessness of lust.

Pulling off and covering my breast, Lily's lips moved back to mine, and we kissed deeply. My hands slid her shirt halfway up her back, exposing her pink bra strap, my fingers dancing along her warm, silky skin. I got dizzy as her tongue twirled along my earlobe. I started to respond.

"What the fuck?" We both turned our heads to look at John standing at the door.

"What the fuck?" he asked again.

"We can... we can explain, umm-"

"Chill," John cut me off. "I don't care. I was just coming up here to get some help from her," he nodded toward Lily.

"Oh, okay," Lily's face flushed. "Gotcha, I'll help." She swallowed hard, then asked, "Give us a sec?"

"Sure," John said, closing the door.

"I'll talk to him," she assured me.

"Okay," I nodded, still breathing heavily. "Trust me?"

"Yeah, of course." She kissed me one more time before leaving.

My mind started tumbling thoughts around like an overloaded dryer, around and around, spitting out scenarios like dirty laundry and none I wanted to happen. It seemed to me every single possible action was John spreading rumors, forcing me out before I was ready. Why wasn't I ready? Was I ashamed? Scared? Or just plain cowardly about being different? But was I really all that different from a straight girl?

Not fearlessly but courageously, I took another swig from my soda and grabbed my purse from beside the chair. I opened it without even thinking, pulled out the crumpled-up plastic baggie, pulled out a pill, and took it with another swallow of soda. I wanted to ease my mind, get away from all the bullshit that I was thinking. I just wanted to relax. I sat back and watched the movie, waiting for the pill to ease my troubled mind.

Matty was wiping the countertop with a handful of brown napkins that were already half-drenched with butter. The bottom half of her shirt was wet and stuck to her stomach; the front of her pants looked as though she'd peed herself.

"Got yourself a mess, huh?" I asked jokingly.

"Damn butter bag busted all over the place." She grabbed another handful of napkins.

I went behind the counter and grabbed my own napkins to help her clean up.

"Well, the next guy that takes me out, I'll be able to ask if he'd like his popcorn with butter or not," Matty said, throwing her dirty napkins in the trash can.

I laughed, "Only you could turn this into something perverted."

"Hey, why not," she smiled. "So, other than this, how was your night?"

"Laid back. You?"

"Good as always. Well, all I did was watch the movie," I grinned.

"Yeah," she agreed.

"Hey, I hate to ask, but," her voice turned into a whisper, "can I get a couple until next check?"

"Yeah, sure thing."

"I hate to get sick again," she shuddered at the thought.

"I gotcha," I said. "What causes that-"

"Withdrawal, baby, hope you never have it."

Our conversation ended as Lily sauntered up to the counter.

"One large popcorn, please," she tried to hold back her smile.

"Funny," Matty said.

"So, Salem, you ready?" Lily asked.

"Yeah," I answered and then covered my tracks by adding, "Thanks again for driving me. I'd hate to walk in this rain."

"No problem," she added, knowing my worries about coming out too early.

"You cool?" I asked Matty.

"Yeah, I got this."

"Alright, well, see ya later." She gave us a half-hearted wave as we turned to go.

Then I remembered I hadn't given Matty her stuff. "Hold on."

"Sure," Lily said.

I went back to the counter, slinging my purse off

my shoulder. I pulled out a pen and a sticky note to make it seem as if I wasn't passing her pills.

"Thanks. Good looking out," Matty said to my back as I walked back toward Lily.

"I forgot to write my number down for her. She lost it," I told Lily. I felt terrible for lying, but could I tell her the truth? Could I tell her I get high? I probably couldn't tell her without losing her, I thought.

"Oh, okay. Come on, let's go to my place."

"Well, Reese Witherspoon is a badass in Freeway, and the Molly Ringwald one is good, but let's go with Sasha Lane. Nothing like a road trip to start the morning."

After we both finished clearing our plates and I washed the dishes, which I had to demand to be allowed to do, we snuggled up on the couch and watched the movie. My phone rang out with a text message about fifteen minutes into the film.

"Ignore it," Lily kissed my neck.

"'Kay," I slid my hand under her shirt and rubbed her stomach, making her nuzzle my shoulder before I leaned down to kiss her lips.

My phone rang out once more about ten minutes later, but I ignored that one as well.

Nearly two hours later, and halfway home, I ran my fingers along the side of my cell phone as I checked the time, nearly overwhelmed by the same feeling I had when I got the texts during the movie that something was out of place. I had intended to just look at the time and go to my apartment, but I felt compelled to check my text messages now instead of waiting until later.

Both were from Matty. The first one was normal enough:

"U holdin? I'm shaky. Please say u got me."

The next made me worry:

"I'm sick. Please pick up."

I dialed her number as soon as I cleared the messages. No one picked up.

Breathe easy...

It seems as though my entire world has fallen at my feet. The foundation that had been strong as stone shifted like sand during a massive breath of wind. What was I supposed to do?

I try so hard to hold back the pain. My jaw clenches, trying to stop the teeth-chattering spasm that wants to erupt as a scream, or a plea, or both. How was I to know?

Breathe easy...

Just breathe easy. I've called three times and sent four text messages to Matty. Where could she be? What is she doing? Simply put: What the fuck?

I slid my sunglasses on in hopes of dodging the morning sunlight, even though it was nearly 10 o'clock. I didn't feel up to embracing the full force of the brightness this close to waking up. I had fallen asleep and taken a short nap during the movie, the restless night finally catching up, but Lily let me use her as a (not too shabby) pillow.

I kept walking, slinging my purse back onto my shoulder every few steps and cursing myself for bringing the damn thing. I was strolling through the parking lot, heading toward the apartment complex, when not only did my purse strap slide down for the billionth time, but my phone rang out with an incoming text. Matty finally responded:

I didn't even bother to reply. I continued toward my apartment. My worries had washed away with her text, but as I neared my door and took her in, I was drowning in concern.

"Oh. My. God," my eyes wide with shock.

Not since seeing my mother bloody and crumpled in my father's arms have I seen anyone else beaten or bruised. Matty's left eye, what I could see of it, was a weird shade of blackish-purple and three-quarters shut.

"What...," I dropped my purse at the door. "What happened?" I must've asked three or four times. I tried to look closer, but she waved me off with a feeble push, trying her best to hide behind her hair. Her lip was split, I noticed, right in the corner. Dried blood stained the hollow of her neck, where I'm guessing she didn't wipe it off.

"Can we just go in?" she mumbled, defeated.

"Sure, sure," I picked my purse up and fumbled with my keys with shaky hands. I took a deep, steadying breath to try and stabilize my trembling.

I pushed the door open with keys still swinging on the knob with my right side, with Matty leaning on my left. I helped her to the couch, my arm wrapped around her waist. I could feel her shivering like a scared puppy. I hustled to retrieve my keys, shut the door, and dropped my purse on the coffee table so I could tend to her quickly. I tried to fetch a glass of water for her, but with shaky hands, I had to fill it up twice. Finally, with a full glass, I went to sit beside her.

"We gotta call someone. We gotta-" I rambled,

getting up to pace back and forth behind the couch.

"No," Matty said without me really hearing.

"We gotta-" I was trying to use my phone, but it looked more like a juggling act.

"No," she said sternly. I could hear the tears in her voice. I could feel her pain as she croaked, "We," she took a breath, "are not calling anyone."

Not believing her reasoning, I said, "What? You have to."

"No," She swallowed, but it looked as if she was swallowing back something that was cutting her throat. She grimaced. "It's nothing. 'Kay? It's nothing."

"What do you mean it's nothing?" I asked, "Look at you."

"I'm sure I look like a model from The Devil Wears Prada."

"You're joking?"

Leaning forward, elbows on knees, she held her head and looked at me as if I couldn't get the hint. She stared at me with a glare burning with tears. "What else can I do? Huh? I was stupid. I fell. End of story."

The tone of her voice and the desperation to end the conversation made me shut up. I sat down.

She leaned down and reached in her shoe, grabbed a plastic baggie that looked like a rock, and threw it at me. "Crush some of those, will ya?"

"Really?" One, I was amazed at how many pills were in the bag. Two, I was amazed she could even think about drugs right now instead of reporting to the police about this incident, but then, looking back at the pills, they were probably the reason why.

Matty was silent for a long time; she seemed to retreat into herself like a DVD player trying to read a scratched disc. Her eyes focused again on me.

"Yeah," she closed her wet eyes, "I just wanna get away."

I was setting up the cartoon for tonight's show, "8 Ball Bunny," where Bugs keeps running into Fred C. Dobbs, the character Bogart played in "Treasure of the Sierra Madre."

While adjusting the reels, I kept letting my mind wander to Matty. Before I had left to come here, I'd told her she was welcome to stay as long as she needed. She said she'd only been a few hours, but I assured her my offer was still on the table.

I was trying to figure out what had happened to her. Seeing her like that made me feel guilty for not answering her call. But was I truly to blame? How did she go from trying to bum some pills to having a sock full? I didn't believe the 'I fell' excuse. Someone hit her, but who? What happened? She got her stuff from Big John, did he do it? If so, why? It could have been her parents. Or maybe even a new dealer?

I tried to focus on my job. Lily was working the snack bar tonight, so I was alone in the booth for the first time in a long time. The movie was a personal favorite of mine from Audrey Hepburn's work, "Wait Until Dark." It just amazed me her performance while dealing with the struggles of divorce from the man who happened to be the producer, having enough stress to cause weight loss, and trying to portray a terrorized blind woman.

Out of the blue, I remembered Hepburn once held the record for having a dress sell for the highest price, that was until Marilyn Monroe stole that crown with her "Seven Year Itch" dress, which sold for nearly $5 million.

Unfortunately, even my vast amount of movie trivia couldn't derail my train of thought. The track was set, and the locomotive kept chugging along to Matty.

But then, without warning, a shiver ran up my spine, and my fingers twitched a couple of times. I swallowed, but a groan escaped nonetheless. My stomach tightened, and I felt bile rise up my throat. I knew this feeling instantly.

I needed a pill. Any pill. Now. But, of course, I wasn't holding. I became aware of the fact I didn't know how I got here. I couldn't remember anything after leaving the booth. "What happened?"

"You fell walking out to the snack bar. I had to get John and Steve to help you in my car. When we got here, you were able to shuffle your way in here with my help," a laugh burst from her, "you should've seen Steve. Oh, the time I had convincing him that you were not high but suffering from very bad food poisoning. Ya know, since that Chan thing, he's been on 'high' alert."

"Yeah," I said weakly. "Could you tell me how or why?"

"Right now, I don't think I could really answer that, honestly. It's not that I don't want to, but I don't really know myself."

"Do you really want to stop?" her eyes stared intently, waiting for my response. "To keep you?"

"Yes," I started crying again. "It-it's just gonna b-be s-so hard."

"I know it is, baby," she kissed me. "I love you."

"I love you too." She kissed both of my eyes, her

hands framing my face. Her fingers slid smoothly down my skin to cup my jaw; then she kissed my mouth. Her eyes glassy from tears, "We'll make it together."

I leaned in with my kiss, my hands wrapping around her neck after traveling up her back. I kept leaning into the kiss, her mouth opening to accept my tongue. Her arms went around my middle, and her hands ran up and down my back. My hands caressed her bare legs, moving up until my fingers touched the denim strands of her cut-off shorts. Her breath was warm against my neck as she placed kisses up to my earlobe then nibbled. Lily's fingertips went under my shirt, and pulled it up and off in one swift motion. With the same skill, she removed my bra. In a tangle of limbs, I helped Lily remove her shirt and bra, then positioned her so she was under me on the couch. The tips of our noses touched, and I went to kiss her lips. Releasing her lips, I let my tongue travel down her neck toward her breasts, where I paused to gently kiss each one. When our eyes locked, I gently bit down on her nipple. Lily's back arched, and I sucked briefly, then ran my tongue over her nipple to soothe the sting. After giving her other breast the same attention, I licked a path toward her navel.

I kissed her stomach and circled my tongue

around her belly button, dipping in and twirling before moving on. Sitting up, I begin to unbutton and slide her shorts down the length of her legs, then off. I leaned over, our faces inches from each other's, each panting and staring, waiting for the other's move. I kiss the corner of Lily's mouth, then run my tongue again down her body to the top of her panties. Lily's hips moved upward in a silent invitation. Her breath caught in her throat as I slid the fabric down agonizingly slow, feeling the prickle of a few days of unshaven hair on my lips until just enough of her was exposed. I pushed my mouth closer, taking all of her in, her scent, her taste. I flicked my tongue across her clit as I pushed her panties the rest of the way down her legs. I raised up long enough for her to kick them off and for me to lean in to kiss her lips once more.

Panties gone, I move between Lily's spread thighs. Her breath hitched as I ran my tongue up and down her folds, tasting, causing her to tighten her legs around me and her fingertips to dig into the back of my neck. Without warning, I slid my tongue in, followed by one, then two fingers. I used the thumb from my other hand to massage her clit, as my fingers moved in and out, my tongue continuously teasing. Lily's breathing became quick, labored pants, then seemed to stop until the point she released a deep moan and came. I continued to lick and tease, all the while feeling her tense up again. I wound her up, and up, and up until she let go with another orgasm.

I planted one more gentle kiss at the edge where her public hair began, then pushed myself up until we were both staring into each other's eyes once more.

It was well into the early morning hours, and we were still naked, snuggling up on the couch with a faded purple blanket thrown over us. A bowl of popcorn was wedged between her legs and a pillow. We had started our movie marathon by checking into 1408, then visiting Shutter Island, now we were watching Under the Skin.

"Here it comes," Lily pointed enthusiastically.

"What?"

"Just look."

"Oh my god," I blurted out with as much fervor as she had.

"She is a bombshell," she moaned and bit her lip.

We both lusted after Scarlett Johansson's birthday suit and wondered where we could buy one.

"Hell, you look much better," I said.

"No way, I think you need glasses."

"What? You have the better features and size.

Hell, you totally steal the show from her, at least to me, you do."

"Shut up," she smacked my side playfully, planted a wet kiss on my lips, and pulled me closer.

We sat and watched the rest of the movie in silence, holding each other and occasionally feeding each other popcorn. Near the end of the movie, the silence was broken as I screamed Lily's name as she made me come with nothing but her thumb.

I felt my heart pour out. I felt my soul cross over, and right then, I knew she was the one I wanted to spend my life with. This right here, right now, was my castle-in-the-sand moment. Each time we were together took away my need to get high, but when I wasn't near her, the tide came, and the wind scattered parts of the castle we built together. If I let it, the drugs will ruin us. I knew this, yet it was so hard not to think of something I'd been doing for so long. I had to choose. I wanted to choose love. Am I strong enough to? I hope I am.

Despite the storms in my mind, worrying over Matty, my job, me, and Lily, my exhaustion consumed me, and I fell asleep fast.

I wanted one of those days you see in the movies where, after a night of lovemaking, the couple only gets out of bed to use the toilet or to get something to munch on before going back under the covers to cuddle.

Unfortunately, the morning wasn't out of a chick flick or directed by John Hughes. Lily did fix another unforgettable breakfast. This time, we both contemplated selling the biscuits to the closest mason in town. We talked about the future, weighing the possibilities and the odds. And, we managed to view "Secret Window" before the morning had to come to an end.

Before I left, and after I washed the dishes, I got a goodbye kiss to sustain me until the next time our lips could touch.

The fresh air was a wonderful therapeutic remedy, clearing my mind, easing my worries, and allowing me to think. I used this time to try and clarify some things that were still blurry in my own eyes. I made an effort to examine everything I could to find my reason to get high. Even a half-hearted reason wouldn't present itself. How did I fix a problem if I didn't know the cause?

The pavement was still dark, damp from last night's rain that I had no idea we'd had while I kept shelter under Lily's blankets. I zipped up my worn-out leather jacket and cursed myself for falling in love with it in the store because it being mid-length left my stomach cold.

Thinking of my own excuse for being an addict made me think of others I knew about. I read that Judy Garland was a victim of Hollywood's predators; her self-image was influenced and constantly criticized by film executives who believed her unattractive. This drove her to drugs and alcohol, and eventually an overdose. There was also Brittany Murphy, who overdosed on over-the-counter medications trying to treat her pneumonia; at least, that was the rumor since she had elevated levels in her bloodstream. And Chris Farley who got to see the release of his "Beverly Hills Ninja" before dying in a nearly identical fashion as his idol John Belushi. There were plenty more, Heath Ledger, who didn't even get to see the premiere of his most iconic role because of drugs.

What reasons did I have? My excuse? Why?

What started out as an amazing cleansing was now a curse. I wanted my mind to stop wandering now. As I neared Asheboro Pawn, I decided to stop in; there was no better way to forget your own troubles than to watch the troubles of others.

The door's opening was accompanied by the owner and her two daughters greeting. "Been a long time," the owner smiled, "many movies for you!"

"Thank you. I hope so. I need some."

I'd recently watched "The Intern" and wanted to see more of Anne Hathaway's work. My eyes ran along the DVD cases, seeking more of the Brooklyn native's roles. I rifled through the titles and came across "Havoc" and "Brokeback Mountain," the former, if I remembered correctly, was her first adult role; the latter also had Michelle Williams, which won me over since I loved "Dawson's Creek." I stumbled upon a Bill Murray I hadn't seen, "Lost in Translation," which also had a stunning Johansson. I found a few other movies, then did the mental debate of actually picking between the ones I wanted to see the most before heading toward the cash register.

Once I was at my apartment, I put my bag of pawn shop purchases on the kitchen table before grabbing a soda out of the refrigerator. I drank the Coke while fixing the coffee maker to work its magic and put some pizza bagels in the microwave. After the pot of java brewed and my food was the right temperature to eat without burning my tongue, I grabbed my plate, cup, and bag of movies, and headed toward the living room. I plucked "Nick & Norah's Infinite Playlist" from its case and sat down to relax, eat and enjoy the movie.

Three cups of coffee, half a plate of pizza bagels, and a couple burps later, I was still enjoying the film.

I was in the process of devouring another bagel when suddenly I burst out laughing, dropping it on the floor.

"Shit." I quickly glanced at the bagel, trying not to miss any of the movie. After a second of thought, I just grabbed the remote and hit the pause button.

I bent down to pick the pizza bagel up (not to eat, but to clean up after myself) and noticed a few pills under the coffee table. I stared at them for a moment, hoping that this was a mirage but reaching out nonetheless with hope that it wasn't a hallucination. My fingertips pulled them from the carpet and gently placed them on the tabletop.

As I looked at them, I thought of Nick and Norah from the movie, who were looking for Where's Fluffy, and that made me think even more about the pills for some reason. It was maybe because I was searching for any excuse to get high.

I don't need them. I grabbed the remote and clicked play. A few minutes into the movie, I once again looked at the pills. I picked one up. Looked at it. I don't need them. I do want them.

Eventually, or better yet, inevitably, I wrapped my other hand around my mug and tossed the pill into my mouth, followed by a swig of warm coffee.

I knew these pills were a vice. I knew that I

promised I'd quit. But as the clock ticked by and the feeling kicked in, I believed it to be worth it. The high (my precious) was worth it as long as the high lasted because when I was high, I didn't care. (Frankly, my dear, I don't give a damn). Was that true? Did I really believe that? What about Lily? I loved her, and I promised her, but these damn pills!

I felt on the verge of a nervous breakdown. I shook with sobs. I wanted Lily, but I also wanted... why was it so hard to break a habit? And why was it so easy to develop one?

The arguing voices in my head were temporarily stilled by a rising tide of need. I needed another pill. I felt an odd sense of thankfulness and guilt as my fingers trembled over another one, picking it up and swallowing it dry.

Looking down at the glass tabletop, I saw my eyes were bright with pain and weariness, but I recognized these things as no more than a surface glitter. Beneath it, I sensed a growing burden and demand that would almost surely become my entire life if it continued to develop with no resolution.

My life was in the balance now; the balance was tipping the wrong way, threatening to flip the entire thing over, and the worst part was no one knew this better than I, but I still believed there was a way to end the constant debate. I knew of one way to at least silence it. I picked up another pill.

I sent a text to Matty:

SALEM: Where u at?

I was still holding my phone when she replied:

MATTY: W/ Big John

A few seconds passed before she sent another text:

MATTY: U can come if you want 2

The average length of a movie trailer is two and a half minutes. Times that by three and that's close to the time it took me to get to Big John's place. I could hear the television blaring through the front door and found myself trying to guess what was being watched before I knocked. I rapped my knuckles against the door but felt stupid as soon as I saw a doorbell. As the door opened it took me a minute to realize it was Big John. He was wearing a bathrobe and, surprisingly, a pair of sunglasses and socks with sandals. His lips curved upward as they stretched into a grin. He motioned me in with a wave of his beer bottle. "Come on in, Matty's in here."

I followed him into the living room where I was surprised at Matty's appearance. She was on the couch with a blanket wrapped around her, and by the look of her bare shoulders, nothing else underneath.

"Salem," she happily slurred, "come on, sit down."

"Did I," I coughed, "did I interrupt something?"

"Nah. I'm crashing here for a bit." She pointed at her face, "ya know, cuz of this."

"Yeah, sure." I felt a little uncomfortable. "She's good company," Big John proclaimed. "But three's a party. Take a squat, Salem." For some unknown reason, I felt dirty. I imagined his eyes behind those glasses' dark lenses, tracing my body. I felt exposed, and this was reinforced when I saw Matty clenching the blanket close around herself.

Looking at Matty I wondered if this was how she really had hoped her life would be like. I wondered if she still had any hope of a better future, even as she sat curled up naked under a drug dealer's blanket.

I know I did. "Uh," I stammered, "I-I think I'll come back later. I can-"

"Nonsense," Big John announced with the exclamation of the silver tray banging the top of the coffee table, putting an assortment of drugs on display.

"Come on, at least stay a little while," Matty said, patting the seat beside her to emphasize her point.

I hesitated only a second before sitting down, but my mind was still in indecision until I saw Big John crushing the pills; then all hesitation vanished.

I was mesmerized by Matty fixing her needle, fascinated by the stream of blood shooting back into the syringe, and I bit my lip with anticipation as she pushed the plunger down, injecting every last drop. Her eyes fluttered with ecstasy. "Yeah, that's it." Big John took the needle from her loose fingers as she slumped back into the cushions. He took an alcohol pad and wiped the needle. He asked me if I'd like some, not with words, but by waving the needle toward me. I shrugged in response. He smiled as I reached out, but suddenly, my cell phone rang with an incoming text message.

It was Lily:

> LILY: <3 Just thinking of u
> ;) <3

I stared at the message, then shook my head. Hope. Hope is the only thing I have left. I was finally choosing Lily. The hope of a better future. "I can't. I gotta go."

"Alright," he said, retrieving the syringe and

placing it back on the tray.

"I'll see you later," I said, looking toward Matty, but she was already teetering on unconsciousness. I made my way to the front door when a hand landed on my shoulder. I turned around quickly and locked eyes with Big John. His lips were slightly parted, his breath loud and rancid, but worse of all, I could read the expression he wore. I shrugged his hands off. "What is it? I gotta go; my friend's expecting me." I hoped my voice didn't betray my emotions.

"Well, you're gonna be late," he whispered. He grabbed my left shoulder and pulled me closer, his right hand reaching around and squeezing my ass cheek harshly. I slammed my fist into his chest and tried to push him off, but in terms of physical strength, I had no chance. "Get off, you motherfu—" He yanked my arm and threw me into the wall of the hallway. I clipped my shoulder on the edge of the entry and felt air burst from my lungs.

I scrambled up on my hands and knees in an attempt to get up, but he kicked between my legs, hitting my stomach with enough force to make me fall back down. I hitched forward, my face scraping against the carpet. I crawled as quickly as I could into the living room.

"Matty!" She only moaned, turned her head, and fell back into a drug-induced slumber.

All of a sudden, I was pressed down, my head sliding across the rug. Caught off guard, I couldn't even try to turn over.

"Stop-" SLAP.

"Please-" SMACK.

My cheek began to twitch as I felt my shirt rise up, exposing my stomach. The firm line on my lips slackened and trembled as I felt my jeans being tugged and heard the fabric holding the button in place tear. My chest hitched once...twice...three times. His rough and calloused fingers dug into my sensitive skin. When I felt him get where he wanted, my mouth opened, and all of my despair and terror came out in one groaning cry.

I came to coughing, and I heard a wheeze escape my nose. I lifted my face off the floor and spat a glob of god-knows-what to get the taste of blood from my mouth. I searched the room while still lying down, not wanting to draw attention but equally wanting to get the hell out of the house. My fingers inched around in search of my pants. I struggled to put them on. My breath hitched when I saw a pair of bloody panties on the floor. They were mine. I gritted my teeth while zipping my jeans. Walking out, I started crying again. I shuffled, stumbled, and wandered my way to the only place I knew to trust: Lily's.

Only when I stood wobbling did I notice the clear night sky with its crescent moon shining brightly. I knocked with a weak fist. I squinted as the porch light flashed on. The door opened quickly with a wide-eyed Lily.

"Where have you been? I've texted you-" her words shut off. Her eyes filled with terror. Her breath gasped as I fell into her arms.

"Oh my god! Salem, breathe easy. Just breathe easy..." These are the last words I remember. 'Breathe easy.'

That's my story, or at least all I can tell you. I remember when I first came to, I was exhausted, still am. I could hardly get my thoughts in order enough to know where I was. Then, I was seized by panic as the fragmented images of him came to me. Have I lost Lily?

So, in these hours inside intensive care, I've been able to think. I mean, really think. I don't see myself as mentally damaged or pathetically weak for my addictions. I think maybe after all of this, I've been made stronger by the turmoil of losing. We don't always get the happy ending we want, but we do have the power to edit the script a little and choose most of the cast. Just like anything else, a movie can be interpreted by anyone who sees it. My own life, if it were on the silver screen, I'd see as a story of not finding what you want but getting what you need.

Life isn't a movie; it isn't written for the big screen; it is reality, and we live it for ourselves and with others. Our choices, we face the consequences of them as well as the people around us, good or bad. At every moment in life, there are choices. And you can choose one thing or the other; even choosing to do nothing is in itself a choice. Right or wrong. Left or right. Choices. Every right choice brings you closer to your best possible path toward true happiness. Every wrong one leads you further and further away from what really matters to you.

These choices in life aren't just decisions that lead to actions but thoughts that lead to beliefs as well. My life today is a sum total of all the choices I ever made. So, all the terrible shit, I made those choices to allow the circumstances to arise to permit the idea that ever crossed his mind. Had I not ever known him, would this still have happened? Or was it Matty who led me to the harder stuff? Or, was it my own doing of ever picking up that joint behind the football field at school?

What I do know now is that my choices led me to Lily. And for that, I would go through all this hell again to find her and what we created together. I am getting the help I need. It reminds me of those lines from a Melanie Martinez song: "Pretending everything is alright is detention." Not any longer; I am not afraid to admit it now.

I lifted my feet as the nurse pushed my wheelchair back toward my room. The police report is over. The nurse changed the bandages on my head, hand, and side, then fluffed my pillow and left a cup of water in easy reach before leaving.

After what feels like forever and a day, the door opens again. Despite the dull headache and the pain, I lifted myself up enough to see her enter. At first, she wasn't looking at me. Her not looking at me concerned me more than hateful words. I couldn't bring myself to break the silence. I wasn't sure what to say. Lily, I love you. Please forgive me.

She came closer, leaned over, and held the back of my neck as though it was as fragile as a porcelain doll. I smelled her hair and her skin as if it were my last. She didn't speak, only kissed me. Her actions spoke the

words. I knew there was still a hole to fill a few frames
left to put in the reel, but they would keep for now.
Now roll the credits and play a happy song.

About the Author

Carietta Dorsch currently lives in North Carolina. She learned of her passion for writing at an early age and hopes to share this gift to the world. She wants nothing more than to gift the type of story that takes you away on a journey and teaches you something about yourself.